MOST WANTED

Also by Kiki Swinson

Wifey

I'm Still Wifey

Life After Wifey

The Candy Shop

A Sticky Situation

Still Wifey Material

Playing Dirty

Notorious

Sleeping with the Enemy (with Wahida Clark)

Heist (with De'nesha Diamond)

Lifestyles of the Rich and Shameless (with Noire)

A Gangster and a Gentleman (with De'nesha Diamond)

Published by Kensington Publishing Corp.

MOST WANTED

KIKI SWINSON
NIKKI TURNER

Dafina
Books

Kensington Publishing Corp.

http://www.kensingtonbooks.com

DAFINA BOOKS are published by

Kensington Publishing Corp.
119 West 40th Street
New York, NY 10018

All Kensington Titles, Imprints, and Distributed Lines are available at
special quantity discounts for bulk purchases for sales promotions, pre-
miums, fund-raising, and educational or institutional use. Special book
excerpts or customized printings can also be created to fit specific needs.
For details, write or phone the office of the Kensington special sales man-
ager: Kensington Publishing Corp., 119 West 40th Street, New York,
NY 10018, attn: Special Sales Department, Phone: 1-800-221-2647.

Dafina and the Dafina logo Reg. U.S. Pat. & TM Off.

ISBN-13: 978-0-7582-8025-1
ISBN-10: 0-7582-8025-4
First Kensington Trade Paperback Edition: October 2013

eISBN-13: 978-0-7582-8027-5
eISBN-10: 0-7582-8027-0
First Kensington Electronic Edition: October 2013

10 9 8 7 6 5 4 3 2 1

Printed in the United States of America

Contents

The Most Wanted Diamonds
Kiki Swinson
1

On Da Run
Nikki Turner
115

The Most Wanted Diamonds

Kiki Swinson

1

Coming Back to Haunt Me

"Hey, baby?" I sang into my cell phone as soon as I heard Sidney's sexy voice come through the line. I could actually picture my husband smiling on the other end of the phone. He always smiled when it came to me.

"Guess where I am? No, silly, I'm not at home butt naked waiting for you." I laughed at his joke. "Seriously, I'm two minutes from the lot. Thought I would surprise you with lunch and a quick midday kitty call," I said seductively.

Sidney sounded excited to hear my voice. He just loved when I did little impromptu things like this. It wasn't always easy finding time to be spontaneous with him being such a busy businessman. He was much older than me, and I guess his previous relationships weren't as much fun. Sometimes I had to pull him out of his shell. It was nothing for me to try to keep him happy, so long as he kept making money.

"Don't worry about what I'm wearing . . . you'll see when I get there," I cooed. He was saying something when my phone line beeped with another call interrupting our sexy talk. I pulled the phone away from my ear and saw that it was my mother. I blew out an exasperated breath. She always knew how to interfere at the wrong times. Sidney was saying something dirty, acting like the dirty old man that he was, but I had to cut him short.

"Look, baby, that's my mother on the other line. Let me holla at her and see what she wants. I'll see you in a few. Be ready for me," I told Sidney. He sounded excited as shit as we hung up.

I clicked over and put on my mental suit of armor. I loved my mother, but she could be a nag and annoying as hell too. It didn't make things easy that she basically lived off of me . . . well, my husband really. The days of living off of me were long gone. I had come into some money, but I'd burned through it just as fast as I had gotten it. My mother had been right there burning up my little windfall with me. I had done some nice things for her because she raised me as a single mother in the rough streets of DC when most mothers were leaving their kids to go smoke crack and shit. Still, my money was gone, and she and I were basically dependents right now. Sidney took care of me, and in return I took care of my mother.

"Yes, ma. What's up?" I answered the line, my voice dull and lifeless. Nothing like how I'd just spoken to Sidney. I wanted her to know I was busy and didn't have a lot of time to yak it up on the phone with her.

"Gigi?!" my mother belted out, damn near busting my eardrum. I pulled the phone away from my ear for a few seconds and frowned. She was bugging! I could hear her yelling my name again. "Gigi!"

"Slow down, lady . . . is everything all right? Why are you yelling?" I asked, concerned. I hadn't heard her all loud like this since she thought she'd hit the lottery a couple of months back. Long story. "You okay?" I asked again.

"Yeah! Yeah . . . everything is just fine. I got some news, baby!" she shrieked excitedly. *You got a damn job and no longer need to live off of us,* was what I was thinking, but I didn't dare say that. Once I realized her high-pitched voice wasn't caused by someone kicking her ass, I calmed down for a few seconds. I let out a long breath waiting to hear some crazy story of hers.

"Okay?" I said expectantly. "What is the news?"

"You will never guess who I spoke to today!" my mother yelped. Before I could even ask who, she volunteered the information. "Warren! I spoke to Warren! Your Warren, baby! He said he is coming home in less than a month and he wants to see us . . . well, really, he wants to see you the most," she said excitedly.

I felt like someone had just punched me in the side of my head. An immediate pain crashed into my skull like I'd been hit. "Warren?" I mumbled, my eyebrows immediately dipping on my forehead. I wished my ears had deceived me. A cold feeling shot through my veins and I almost dropped the phone and crashed the car. My heart immediately began thumping wildly, and cramps invaded my stomach like an army going in for the kill.

"Yes! Warren! He is getting out early on some kind of deal

or good behavior . . . something like that! Isn't that good, Gigi?!" my mother continued.

I was speechless. I couldn't even think. Flashes of Warren's face started playing out in front of me. The last time I saw him haunted me now.

"You there, Gigi?" my mother inquired, her voice changing as she must've realized her news wasn't so good. I swallowed hard before I could get the words to come out of my mouth. I cleared my throat because the lump sitting in the back of it made it hard for me to talk. I could feel anger rising from my feet, climbing up to my head.

"How the hell did Warren get your new number?!" I asked through clenched teeth. My voice had no problems now. My nostrils flared and I gripped the steering wheel so hard veins erupted to the surface of the skin on the back of my hand.

"When I moved you from the fucking hood in Southeast DC, I told you to leave that shit behind altogether!" I chastised. "What is wrong with you?! You just couldn't leave well enough alone!" I barked some more. I was full on sweating now. My head was spinning a mile a minute. She had no fucking idea what she had done. "Whose side are you on?!" I screamed.

My mother was quiet at first. I'm sure she was looking at the phone like it was an alien from outer space. I guess she didn't know how to process my anger. She also didn't know the details of my history with Warren after our arrests, which probably confused her even more. It really wasn't her fault. My mother had always liked Warren for me. I mean, he had scooped me up out of the hood and given me a life my mother knew she could never give me. He didn't spare a dime when it came to her either. Sometimes my mother had seemed more enamored with Warren than me.

It was understandable given her history with men. As a kid, I had watched my mother go from one no-good bastard to another. My father had left as soon as I was born . . . typical hood story. My mother had always tried to find that perfect man, so most of my life her bedroom was like a revolving door. There would be one dude this month and another dude the next month. She would always come to me and say, "Gianna, I think this one is going to be your step daddy for sure this time. Baby, we gonna have a good life if it's the last thing I do." Pretty sad when I think back on how desperate my mother had been to find real love. I had watched niggas beat my mother, take her money, steal our TVs, and leave her so depressed she wouldn't get out of bed for weeks.

I was determined to be better than that when I grew up. I wanted to finally give my mother that good life, but school and hard work wasn't in my DNA.

When I met Warren, he became my security blanket. He bought me food, clothes, and eventually, shelter. My mother was love struck herself. I would even catch her blushing sometimes when Warren would come to the house and joke around with her. I don't know why her staying in touch with Warren came as such a shock to me now. I always knew she'd probably pick him over me in a close call situation anyway. Plus, I had never told her what I'd done to him after he and I got knocked riding dirty. After Warren went to federal prison, I played the whole distraught girlfriend role in front of my mother, never letting on to the truth of the situation. She had seemed torn even then.

The news my mother had just dropped on me had me reeling. I started calculating shit in my head. I had been given a false sense of security thinking Warren was going to do much longer in prison. I didn't think he would be getting out so soon. . . . It had only been four years and according to the information I got, Warren had been charged with all types of gun charges, RICO shit, and the whole nine yards. I was under the impression from the feds that Warren would have the book thrown at his ass when he got sentenced.

Someone had fucking lied to me. This was definitely not part of the plan I had hatched back then. Even still, I thought for sure I had made provisions where Warren would never find me. I had changed my name slightly—no longer going by Gianna, I was now simply Gigi. I had moved out of DC, finally settling in country-ass Virginia, and started living the quiet, kept life as the wife of a fucking old rich dude, who technically could be my father. It would take my mother to fuck that all up!

"Ma . . . how did Warren get your phone number?" I asked again, finally able to calm myself down. My jaw rocked feverishly waiting for her answer. I was praying it wasn't her. I was hoping deep inside Warren had just paid a private investigator or some other Lifetime movie type shit.

"Gigi, when we moved from DC, I stayed in touch with Warren. I thought you would get over being mad at him one day and get back with him. I didn't know you were going to marry so fast. Warren was the only man who had ever done anything good for us and I felt obligated to him. He didn't have any family, so I wrote him letters and sent him packages. Not like you . . . you just got a new man and moved on," she replied.

All of my hopes of my mother NOT being the culprit who blew my cover were dashed. I wanted to scream at the top of my lungs. What a dumb bitch! How fucking stupid can you be?! I couldn't say those words, but I sure as hell was thinking them. Panic hit me like a wrecking ball going into a building at top speed. Warren was the last person on earth I wanted to see or hear from right fucking now. I had to breathe slowly through my mouth to calm down enough to keep talking to my mother. I also had to pay attention to the road.

"What have you told him about me?!" I inquired loudly. My voice quivered just thinking about ever seeing Warren again. This was definitely not what I had planned. Again, I silently hoped that my mother had never discussed me with Warren.

"Everything. He knows you're married. He said he is happy for you. He knows you are doing well living here in Virginia Beach with your new husband. I didn't see the problem. The man is locked up and he was still asking about you. I think he always loved you, Gianna. All I can say is sorry, but Warren seemed very happy for you," my mother said apologetically. Something like a cord just snapped inside of me. I was literally coming apart at the seams listening to her.

"You are stupid! You had no right telling him my business! He is my ex and you don't know what the fuck I went through with him because I never told you! Just because you would do any fucking thing just to say you had a man doesn't mean

I grew up to be like you!" I boomed, the cruel words hurling from my mouth like hard rocks. I breathed out a long, hard windstorm of breath.

"Did you also tell him who I am married to? Anything about where I live? Or maybe you gave him my fucking social security number while you were at it?" I asked, trying to sound as calm as I could. It wasn't working; the base in my voice was deep and intimidating.

"Well, excuse me! I thought you would want him to know how well you were doing now seeing that he almost caused you to go to prison right along with him. He didn't even sound like he was interested in getting back with you at all. His questions were all general . . . seemed to just want to know you were all right. I'm sorry if you feel like I did something wrong, but the last time I checked I don't have anything to hide," my mother retorted.

I immediately felt guilty for calling her stupid. I had to try and pull myself together. It wasn't her fault.

She was right. She had no idea what had happened, and maybe she just wanted Warren to know that despite the jeopardy he'd put me in four years earlier, I was doing just fine. There were a few minutes of awkward, eerie silence on the phone line. My mother wasn't the quiet type, so I knew the silence meant she was truly at a loss for words.

"I gotta go," I said. I didn't give her a chance to say a word. I just hung up the phone. A loud horn blaring behind me almost caused me to drive off the road. I swerved my car a little bit to keep from hitting others.

"What the fuck?!" I screamed, looking into my rearview mirror. I swerved onto the shoulder of the road. The string

of cars behind me passed by, drivers cursing at me and laying on their horns. I was shaken up. I clutched my chest. I
had been so distracted by what she was telling me that I was
driving slow as hell, holding up traffic. The news from my
mother had fucked me up so badly I couldn't even drive. I
put my car in Park and sat there for a few minutes.

"Warren is coming home early and knows where I am,"
I said out loud as if I had to convince myself that what I'd
heard was true. My insides churned and I felt like I had to
throw up. My legs rocked in and out feverishly. I could see
the snarl on Warren's face as clear as day in my mind's eye.
I knew him so well. I knew how he was when it came to shit
like loyalty too. I had made a promise to him that I hadn't
kept. I had also seen Warren's wrath firsthand. There was
no way he would just let go of what I had done to him. I
could hear him speaking to me now. "No matter what, just
never cross me. I can live with everything else. Just never
betray me." Warren had said those words to me on several
occasions. The same words over and over, he never changed
it up. Each time he had said them, in return I promised him
that I'd always be loyal, never cross him. I had sworn. I had
pledged my allegiance to him. But then I'd turned around
and committed the worst Judas act of treason against him.

"Fuck!" I screamed, slamming my fists on my steering
wheel until they hurt. "Fuck! Gigi! What the fuck have you
done?! What the fuck are you going to do now?!" I yelled
out loud. Where Warren and I came from, what I had done
was a cardinal sin. In any hood I knew of, snitching and
stealing were both acts as heinous as raping a child or killing
your own parents. That is how seriously street niggas took

it. Most of the niggas I knew, Warren included, lived by the death before disloyalty creed. I was terrified just thinking about the consequences. Maybe he'd shoot me execution style right in front of my mother. Maybe Warren would torture me with battery acid and jumper cables before finally putting me out of my misery. I could only imagine. I closed my eyes and all I could do was think back to how things had gone so wrong. How we'd gone from being so happy—the hood's Prince William and Kate—to being the hunter and the hunted. I kept thinking. Thinking. Something I had tried to avoid doing for four years now. I couldn't help it. My mind went back.

2

In This Together

Washington, DC, 2008

Warren sat on the all-white, butter-soft leather sofa, in just his wife beater and boxers, flipping the channels on the sixty-five-inch flat-screen television that covered the wall in front of him. I stomped over to him, my cell phone in hand ready for whatever. I wore only a pink and black Victoria's Secret lace bra and thong set. I stood my beautiful ass right in front of him, blocking his view of the basketball game he'd finally settled on. I jutted my arm out and put my cell phone screen right in his face. Warren looked up at me like I had just slapped him. I didn't give him a chance to say shit before I went in on him.

"So who is this bitch now, Warren? I mean, she keeps on calling my fucking cell phone and texting me talking shit! Why do I have to go through this shit all of the time!" I screamed as Warren looked at me like I was crazy.

I had been with him three years and the bitches were still

hovering like flies around shit. I mean, every chick in Southeast wanted Warren. It wasn't because of his looks or his ripped abs and smooth black skin either. He may have thought it was what he called his "sweet dick," but I knew better. Nope, it was his fat-ass pockets. It was what had attracted me to him, so I already knew why so many bitches wanted him too. Warren had been known as that nigga running the streets in the Trinidad section of DC forever. He was a man of few words, but his aura and swag spoke for itself. He was the type of dude who changed his car monthly, never wore the same Prada sneakers or fitted cap twice, and kept a knot of money in his pocket that another nigga wouldn't dare try to rob from him. I was attracted to Warren's swag more than his facial features when I'd met him in Love nightclub. He was average looking, nothing super fine about him, but he didn't have to be super fine in the face because, just like Jay-Z, Warren's swag made up for whatever he lacked in looks department. His whole style just screamed, "I'm rich, bitch!" And that shit made him fine all the same. But as with every get-money nigga, being with him also came with a lot of fucking headaches. I received calls from bitches, almost three times a day sometimes, claiming to be fucking him. I had to keep changing my number and without fail they would get the new number. I was always questioning whether they would look in his phone while he was asleep in their beds and get my number. Of course, he always denied it. Warren was so smooth he always ended up making me feel like I was the crazy one. I would not move out of his face until he acknowledged my damn concerns.

"C'mon, G-money . . . why is you bugging me about the

next bitch for? Yo ass is here with me . . . walking around the crib we live in together. Just finished riding this dick into the night. You the one that be riding through the streets in the front seat of my whips like the queen bitch for all those hoes to see. So what's the damn problem?" Warren asked smoothly. He was the only person who called me G-money and I liked it. I kind of smiled inside every time he said it even when I was mad at him. Warren said he gave me that nickname because when I was with him I always looked like a bag of money.

"Just be a queen and don't worry about shit else. Now lean yo ass over here and give ya daddy a fucking kiss." He made me all mushy inside. Even when I tried to be mad, I couldn't stay mad at his smooth ass.

"I'm just saying, Warren, you need to call off these bitches, because it gets tiring. I just want a day where I don't have nobody calling me and stuff," I said softly in my best baby voice. I didn't give his ass no kiss. I wanted him to know I wasn't feeling him. But that didn't last long. Warren grabbed me and pulled me down onto the couch. He kissed me so deep and passionately all of my troubles seemed to melt away. I was so in love with Warren that no matter what he did, I could never imagine my life without him. After he held me tightly for a few minutes, I felt safe and secure. I wasn't going to say shit else about it.

"Let's go to dinner, G-money. Let's go riding through the streets and shit on these starving ass bitches who keep calling you," Warren said. I jumped up excitedly. I loved to go out on the town with my man. I was thinking I could probably convince him to take me to buy a new piece of jewelry or a bag . . . one of the many guilt gifts I'd received from Warren over the years.

We hit the streets hard that night. We both wore all black with our matching Rolex watches the only shine gleaming from our wrists. I wore little to no makeup; my skin was so flawless I hardly needed any. I was definitely a less is more type chick. My hourglass shape, caramel skin, perky D-cups, and long legs didn't need much to make a statement. I never wore weave, my hair was thick, long, and naturally beautiful. Many of the jealous bitches whispered that I had weave, but I knew the truth. Warren paid me many compliments. I think he knew he had a trophy chick on his arm just as much as I knew I had a sponsor on mine.

As we drove through the streets of DC on our way to dinner, I felt real good. I had forgotten all about the chick who kept blowing up my phone. I watched the streets from my perch as Warren's number one and it felt good as hell too. Warren was right about what he had told me when I confronted him. Through the darkly tinted windows of his Mercedes G-Wagon, I could see the envious eyes of all the starving bitches who wanted him so badly. I was thinking they'd probably sell their kids and kill their mama to be me right then. I rolled my window down slightly and smirked at them. I wanted them to see me as Warren's bitch for life. I was definitely shitting on them. I felt warm and fuzzy inside just knowing they wanted to sit where I was sitting.

Warren and I rode in silence for a few minutes. I know he saw me teasing those hoes. I was lost in thought daydreaming about the day I wouldn't have to worry about no other bitch trying to steal my spot on the throne. Warren was bopping to his rap music and all seemed well. The next thing I knew, my body and my neck were being violently jerked around and I heard the tires of the truck screeching like we were on a racetrack. I formed my mouth into an O, but I couldn't even get my words out. My eyes shot wide open as I noticed that the G-Wagon was moving like a fucking rollercoaster ride. I even broke a nail tip trying to hold on to the door for support.

"Oh! That nigga had the nerve to show up back on these streets! Niggas is bold these days, huh? I got something for that ass!" Warren growled. The car whipped around again so hard I bumped my head on the window. Warren was still mumbling about niggas not knowing who they were fucking with and he ain't the one to be fucked with.

"Who? What? What the fuck, Warren?!" I screeched, confused as hell. Before Warren could even answer he was throwing that shit in Park and the next thing I knew, he was out of the truck in a flash. Finally getting my bearings, I followed Warren with my eyes. I knew the way he was moving that it couldn't be something good. I watched in horror as Warren ran up on an unsuspecting dude who stood amid a bunch of guys with his back turned. Warren was on him within a few seconds. The crowd he was in scattered like roaches when the lights come on. I could see the dude put his hands up in defense, terrified. It didn't take him long to realize he had nowhere to run or hide. The guy's efforts to ward off Warren were futile to say the least. There was no defending himself now as Warren went in on the dude like a madman. Warren's rage was apparent to everybody on the streets who had a front-row seat to the show about to go down.

"Where you been, nigga?! Huh?! You thought you could run!" I heard Warren barking from where I sat inside the car. I couldn't even hear what plea the dude was trying to cop, but I could tell he was scared as shit. Warren took a gun from his waistband. My jaw dropped open because I thought Warren was going to shoot that dude right there on the street. Warren was smarter than that, but he drove the butt of that gun up against the guy's head with the force of a fucking tornado. Even I winced just watching it. I could only imagine the pain associated with that first hit.

"What, nigga! What?!" Warren barked. "You thought it was all good! You wanted to show your ass after I let you eat out here on these streets?! You tried to play me like I was a fucking chump?!" Warren was like a demon possessed. After the first gun butt, the guy's head had split open. The gash was so big I swore I could see his brains. Blood and gray gushed out of the guy's face and head. I cringed as I felt vomit creeping up my esophagus. I hated the sight of blood. Warren didn't seem fazed by that shit either.

"You thought I wasn't gon' find out?! Huh, nigga! You know who the fuck I am 'round this, muthafucka! Stealing from me is like denouncing God. . . . I'm God around here, motherfucker! I got the power to send you straight the fuck to hell!" Warren said through tightly clenched teeth as he continued to wail on the defenseless dude. Warren's entire face was like a monster's face, balled up into a hard scowl. The guy was crying like a little girl after he had taken hit after hit. He was literally begging for his life. I think I even saw the nigga piss on himself. Every time the dude opened his mouth, Warren hit him in it even harder than the time before. After about the third time, I could see that man's teeth dropping from his lips like Chiclets. Blood was everywhere. It was a complete mess.

I had to finally turn my face. I could actually feel that man's pain, and suddenly I had an instant headache. Warren continued to pound the guy in the head until the guy finally relented. He crumpled to the ground like a deflated balloon, no longer able to stay on his knees. I couldn't even look back over at the scene as Warren made a mess of that dude's face.

No one on the streets dared to try and stop Warren or come to the guy's defense. Everybody knew who Warren was, and now, just like me, they knew what he was capable of. Warren didn't have to worry about the police either. In the Trinidad section of DC, the cops only came when it was absolutely necessary—like if they thought something might make the news. Besides, the residents there were totally against snitching, so Warren knew he didn't have to be concerned about anyone calling the cops either. It was the first time I'd ever seen Warren like that. I had never witnessed his wrath to that extent.

When Warren started back toward the truck, I swear I could see the devil dancing in his eyes. Those shits flashed red like someone had lit a fire inside of them. Something inside of me was literally shaking and I could not keep my teeth from chattering. I had to actually put my hands under my thighs to keep those shits from trembling so much. Warren slid back behind the steering wheel with blood on his hands and all over his shirt. The smell of the fresh blood on Warren reminded me of raw meat gone bad. I had to put my hand over my nose to keep myself from hurling. I was terrified and shocked at the same damn time. I didn't dare say a word. I didn't even recognize the man sitting next to me. He had never been anything but gentle and loving toward me. But right then, I was scared to even breathe around him. I just remained quiet. I figured I'd let him calm the hell down before I even tried to speak to him.

After what seemed like an eternity of eerie silence in the car, Warren started speaking. I widened my eyes and looked over at him. I wasn't about to interrupt him either.

"G-money . . . why niggas try to test me? They ain't ask about me out here?" Warren asked.

Obviously he wasn't looking for answers to those questions.

"Let that nigga's face be a lesson to anyone who saw that shit. That's what happens when you try to steal from me. That shit applies to any human walking this fucking planet. These niggas ain't about this life! I am this life!" Warren huffed, his nostrils flaring like a bull seeing red.

I was still silent. Too struck to speak. Lost for words. However you wanted to characterize it, I wasn't saying shit. There was nothing I could say that would calm him down and nothing I could do to quell the alarming fear that flitted through my stomach right then.

"Damn . . . now I gotta head back on the fucking highway to go change these clothes. I should make that nigga buy me a new pair of sneakers too. I gotta throw these brand-new Pradas in the damn garbage. Ain't that about a bitch?! Don't worry, G-money, we still going to grab our food. I'ma go change it up and then we on our way. This shit was just a small setback, baby girl," Warren said like it was nothing. He was worrying about changing clothes and throwing a new pair of sneakers in the garbage after he had just fucking put a man as close to death as that? That was real crazy to me. Warren showed no remorse.

I kept staring at the side of Warren's face in astonishment. I was looking for the least bit of remorse or caring. Nothing. I saw no signs that he could care fucking less. In fact, strangely, Warren was back to the same cool, calm, collected dude that I knew. Most people couldn't just fucking do something like that and be all regular right afterward. It was like beating someone half to death was a regular task for Warren. That day was the first time that a small twinge of fear of him sprang up inside of me. I don't think it ever really went away.

3

Gotta Have Trust

It was about two months after I'd seen Warren basically obliterate a dude's face with the handle of a gun that shit got critical for us. Life was easy for the most part until one fateful day, but as usual, shit always has to change. I always slept later than Warren. I don't know if it was the fact that most nights he wore my pussy out so bad I'd be in a coma the next day, or if it was just the constant paper chase that Warren was on that got him up so early every day. That day, Warren had come into our bedroom all frantic, shaking the bed to make sure I knew he meant for me to get the fuck up. Mind you, this was a man who never really broke a sweat over shit. He handled business and life the same way—calm, collected. Except when someone crossed him. So I knew shit was serious when his voice was a few octaves higher than I was used to.

"G-money! Get up. C'mon, get up . . . sleep is the cousin of death," Warren huffed while he used his muscular thigh to shake the bed. I swiped at his leg letting him know I wasn't a happy fucking camper that he was waking me up so violently. "G-money! Sit up! Some shit came up and I need you to ride with me today!" Warren huffed. Warren's voice was kind of a mix between slight panic and desperation. Still groggy with sleep, I sat up slowly, confused. I hated to be jolted out of sleep like that. That was the surest way for me to have a fucking headache all day long.

"Mmm," I moaned, turning my head away from where he stood, letting him know I wasn't happy with being woken up like that.

"C'mon, I ain't got time to hear your mouth about sleep. Sleep when you're fucking dead, now get up," Warren said, shaking the bed with his leg again. I could feel heat rising from my damn feet to my head. He was pissing me off. I huffed and puffed, but I finally got all the way up. "What is it! What are you waking me up for!" I snapped. My morning breath was fierce. I wished I could blow it straight up his nostrils to get him the fuck away from me. Warren started pacing. That surprised me too. He never showed any signs of nervousness before. Pacing was not his style at all.

"Yo! Obviously I'm waking you up for a reason! This is important, G-money. I have to have you do me this real big solid today," Warren said seriously as he kept his feet moving. I looked at him as if to say spit it out already. He took the cue.

"I set up a meeting with some real, real important cats to buy something off me. These is not your regular around the way cats. . . . I'm talking internationally known muthafuckas. I can't let this shit slip through my fingers. Ant was supposed to conduct the transaction on my behalf, but this nigga Ant got caught up real bad. He fucked around and got into it with baby moms and caught a quick DV charge. That nigga hot right now and I can't send him. I can't afford for no police to be on that nigga's ass. This shit is real important, G-money. It has to be done today. I don't trust nobody else but me and that nigga Ant to get it done. And I ain't tryna let this deal go because it is just the first of many that's gon' make me some real cake. I'm talking 'bout the kind of cake that's gon' be our retirement fund . . . get us out this fucking hood, put us on an island somewhere and set us up for life."

Warren was rambling. My mind was reeling as he spoke. What exactly was he asking me to do? I knew the situation was serious because he hardly ever told me his business like that. He had always preached that the less I knew about his lifestyle and business, the better off I'd be if the boys in blue ever tried to pull that polygraph bullshit on me. This was a first, but believe me, I was all ears when he started talking about setting us up for the future. I liked to hear plans for the future that included me.

"What you want me to do?" I asked, my voice still gruff and filled with sleep as I ran my hand under the covers trying to find my robe to cover my naked body. Warren stopped pacing and turned toward me. The expression on his face was serious. More serious than his normal bad-boy frown. He walked over and sat down next to me on the bed. His voice was low and steady. Sexy!

"Look, all you gotta do is sit in the car and look pretty. You can do that shit well, can't you? Pssh, why am I even asking the prettiest chick in DC that question? I know you know how to play your position, G-money, right?" Warren answered my question with a question of his own. He was being a smart ass and I could tell he was kind of frustrated by me asking him for details, but shit, I wanted to know what all this little transaction was going to entail. I guess he could tell by the look I wore on my face that I wasn't fully satisfied with his previous explanation.

"Like I said . . . for you it's just a ride along. See, the Jake ain't gon' really fuck with me if I got a lady in the car. You know how that shit is. They see me alone. . . . I'm a suspect. If I'm with a chick, they'll just think we going for a nice brunch or some shit. The chances of them stopping me with you in the car all dressed up and shit is slim to none. I have heard of niggas riding dirty all the way down I-95 and never getting clocked just cuz a chick was in the car looking fancy," he explained.

It was like a lightbulb had gone off in my mind. Okay, so it clicked. He wanted to use me as a decoy to keep the police away. I twisted my lips and curled my face up into a frown. I thought that was a dumbass idea. Since when did the police care if a black chick was in a car that they wanted to pull over after racially profiling the shit? Especially those fucking Virginia state troopers who were known to be racist pigs. Warren saw my face and made a face of his own.

"But what if they still decide to pull you over anyway? I mean . . . I hear about chicks getting caught up all the time in the car playing that ride-or-die chick shit. I also hear about them getting fucking longer sentences than the dudes," I said, concern lacing my words. Those words were like blight as soon as they left my mouth. Like I had put the bad luck whammy on us. Warren was on his feet in a flash.

"Yo! Don't be speaking negative shit into existence, G-money!" Warren immediately yelled at me. I jumped and when he saw that he had startled me, he quickly softened his voice. He needed me, so he wasn't trying to ruffle no feather. "We gon' be good. I ain't never gonna do shit to put you in harm's way . . . believe that, baby girl. Once we get near the spot, I'm gon' put you some place safe . . . like a mall or something nicer like a spa . . . then I'ma go do the business and come get you after the fact. After I have that cake in hand. As a matter of fact . . . I'm telling you I'm gon' make enough cake that wherever you go you can buy whatever you want. I don't care how much it cost. I just need you to be focused right now and say that you gon' do me this one," Warren assured, finally sitting down on the bed next to me again. Warren had said some key words that I'm sure he knew would get my gears going. Shit! My eyes lit up like a kid at Christmas. I was no longer tired, worried, or thinking about the consequences. All that nigga had to say was shopping, spa, and whatever I wanted. All that sounded like music to my ears. I was a chick who came from nothing, so admittedly material things were more important to me than a lot of other shit. I was more concerned with showing bitches in my old hood that I had come up than going to school or finding a job. It was just the way it was at the time. I hadn't even ever put a dime of the money Warren gave me in the bank.

"That's all you had to say! You know I'ma take one for the team and ride with you!" I exclaimed. Warren immediately smiled and shook his head up and down.

I hopped my ass off of the bed and ran straight for the shower. I set the oversized rain showerhead and got in. Before long, Warren followed me into our all marble and glass luxury shower. The inside was big enough for four adults, so he and I had plenty space to shower together. I smiled when he came in with his sexy-ass body moving close to mine. I chuckled just thinking about how much game this nigga really had. He always knew how to get my ass buttered up for whatever. Dick and money—the fastest ways to my heart. Warren's presence caused a tingly feeling to take over my whole body. This dude still made me giddy.

"I knew you was my ride-or-die chick the first time I laid eyes on you," Warren said seductively as he came up behind me and grabbed a handful of my titties. I could feel his hard dick rubbing on my ass and that made my pussy jump with excitement. Even without the water from the shower, my pussy was immediately soaking wet with my own juices. I closed my eyes as Warren explored my body with his hands.

"You knew from day one? Please, you ain't know shit. You just knew I had a fat ass, nice titties, and a bomb-ass pussy that you wanted to get up inside of," I said through a big grin. I put my hands on top of his as he caressed me gently. A warm feeling engulfed my entire body. It was love, I was sure of that. I let a small puff of air escape my lips. I was already in ecstasy and Warren had barely touched me. Our connection was electric for sure. The water cascading over us, plus the steamy bathroom made the whole scene sexy as hell. Warren kissed on my neck and ran his tongue over my shoulders as he pinched my areolas just enough for me to feel it, but not enough to hurt. I closed my eyes and let the tingling feeling take over my body. One thing was for sure, he knew my weak spots—my neck and my tits set me on fire every time. Warren took full advantage of both places on my body. I was fucking loving every minute of it. Warren was making me weak with all of his kisses and soft bites. I let out a soft moan and bit down into my bottom lip.

"What you want? Huh? Let me hear you. Tell me . . . beg me," he whispered in my ear.

The heat of his breath on my ear and neck almost made me fall out. My pussy was throbbing like it had a heart of its own now. My mouth was watering too. I was longing to feel his swollen dick inside of me. I swear Warren could've fucked me every night and it still wouldn't have been enough. He had the best dick I had ever experienced in my life. Not only was he blessed with a hunk of meat that would make bitches kill for it, he knew what to do with it too. I reached back and tugged on his jewel, letting him know it was time to stop playing and lay that shit on me. Fuck all the foreplay bitches be crying about. I always wanted to bypass that and have Warren straight pile-drive me with that pole he was working with.

"Give it to me, daddy," I moaned, grabbing for it again. He moved back a little so I couldn't reach it. He was definitely teasing me. I was too fucking hot and horny to be playing games with his ass.

Warren let out a deep laugh. "You want that? How bad you want it? Let me hear? How bad?" he whispered teasingly.

I let out a long breath and shook my head from side to side.

"How bad you want that? I'm not giving it to you until you tell me . . . beg me, I said," Warren huffed.

My jaw was rocking feverishly. I was like a fiend waiting for a damn hit from my dealer. "I want it real bad. Fuck me . . . please, daddy, fuck me real good," I said breathlessly.

"You asking me or you telling me?" he said forcefully.

Damn, I loved when he got like that with me. Every experience was different with Warren. Sometimes he was forceful, other times he was gentle. I never knew what to expect, but no matter what he did, I was always overwhelmed.

"I'm begging, daddy. I'm on my hands and knees begging for that dick," I replied, trying to get another handful of his manhood. Before I could touch him again, Warren spun me around and forced me up against the shower wall with a shove. I let out a short gasp, but I complied with him. I let him lift me off my feet with his strong arms. I completely submitted to him. The water was hitting his back and pouring over my face. I braced my back flat against the wet tile on the wall and Warren lifted both of my legs until they were around his waist. I was waiting for him to give me that dick.

"Tell me again what you want," he whispered, nestling

his face into my neck. He was playing around too long. I was getting a little frustrated. "You, daddy . . . I want all of you," I replied forcefully. Water ran over my lips and into my mouth as I spoke. He moved his head and forced his face into my chest. He took in a mouthful of my left titty and sucked it hard. Stabs of heated sparks ran through my entire body. "Yesss!" I hissed, tightening my thighs around him.

Warren went in on my breasts, licking and suckling. That shit was driving me crazy! I dug my nails into his back in response. He sucked hard and at the same time he reached down with his other hand and grabbed his dick. I locked my legs even tighter around him so that I wouldn't slip. Warren swiped the hard head of his cock over my wet pussy a few times before he finally found my hotbox. "This what you want!" he growled as he drove his thick meat deep up into me.

"Ah," I let out a gasp. That shit hurt so good.

"This what you want? I asked you," Warren huffed as he slammed his hips into my pelvis.

"Yes!!" I screamed out. Damn, that dick was so good. The pressure from his pelvis being on my clitoris was all too much. I could feel my back slipping off the wet wall, but I didn't even worry, I just knew Warren wasn't going to let anything happen to me. I felt like my loins would explode. He grinded his waist into my pelvis until it felt like I could feel his dick in my abdomen over and over again. That shit felt so good that I was coming in minutes. "Arrrgg," I growled. I bit into Warren's neck like a vampire. I couldn't help it. That was how hard I climaxed. Warren laughed at me as I climaxed twice in a row. My pussy was sloppy wet, which made the sensation of his dick even more intense.

"Damn, that was fast," he said. I felt kind of embarrassed, but he knew how fast he could make me cum. Warren took me down off the wall and turned me around so that my plump ass was facing him. "My turn now," he said as he pushed me until I was bent over at the waist. I bit my lip again. I just loved this man so fucking much. I don't think no one else could fuck me like that.

Warren slapped my ass until it stung. Then he took me from behind like a horny dog would take a bitch. I planted my hands on the back shower wall for support and let my man pile-drive me to ecstasy again. The sound of our skin slapping together was music to my ears. I loved every minute of being with him. We had been through so much together. The deal was sealed. I decided that no matter what he had asked me to do, I was going to do it.

"You a rider, huh?" Warren huffed as he rammed me harder and harder.

"Fuck yeah!" I belted out. "I'ma ride for you no matter what!" I promised, my words coming out choppy from being rammed so hard. The words may have been choppy, but they were so sincere coming out of my mouth.

"No matter what?" he repeated for assurance.

"No matter what! I swear!" I yelled as he went crazy digging into me harder and harder. The next thing I knew, Warren was exploding inside of my pussy.

"Agggh," he panted. He even climaxed calmly. I almost

collapsed onto the floor of the shower. He had made me fucking weak in the knees. Warren laughed at me again. He extended his hand to help me get up.

"I done wore that pussy out, huh?" he joked.

That was for damned sure. He had worn my pussy and my entire body out. I looked at him and slapped him on his ass playfully. "Don't be so confident," I told him. But he and I both knew he was right. I was done after those two nuts. Warren seemed like he still had all of his damn energy. I hated that. His dick was even still hard. One day I promised to fuck him until that dick couldn't get hard anymore.

"Get ya mind right, G-money. We gotta wash our asses and get out of here. We got some business to take care of . . . right, ride or die?" he told and asked all in one. I smiled at that man. I was all in by then.

"Right," I said with renewed spirit. I collected myself and we soaped each other's bodies. When I touched his dick, I was tempted to fuck him again, but I knew we had something very important to do. We got out of the shower, dried off, and went back into the bedroom.

For some reason, while I began picking out my outfit, the seriousness of our mission started settling in my mind. I guess it was the same for Warren. We got dressed in complete silence. It seemed like neither one of us wanted to be the first to speak about the task at hand. I know for me I was thinking about all kinds of negative shit that could happen. I kept my thoughts inside, though. Like he had told me earlier, I wasn't trying to speak no negative shit into existence. That still didn't change the fact that I was fucking thinking all kinds of crazy negative shit. At one point, I even had to shake my head to try to get those funky thoughts to go away. Regardless of how tentative I was feeling, I still got all pretty, like Warren had told me to do. We smiled at each other nervously as we passed one another to finish up. There was a lot of nervous tension in the room. I know for me, I had butterflies like a muthafucka, but I was hiding it. Warren and I put on our clothes—him a pair of dark blue True Religion jeans, a Hundreds T-shirt, and his beige Louboutin sneakers. I put on a Bebe maxi dress that was simple but close fitting so it hugged my shape. I topped it all off with some BCBG espadrilles and an Yves Saint Laurent clutch. Warren and I put on our matching his and hers oyster shell Gucci shades and headed out of his house hand in hand. Although I was nervous like hell, I still felt like the luckiest girl in the world that day. Just being with the one you love had a way of making you feel like that. Too bad I was none the wiser that the luck would run out quicker than I thought.

"You the baddest bitch in DC when you get dressed," Warren complimented. I looked at my reflection in the mirror and I had to admit, I wasn't so damn shabby. I cleaned up nicely. My long, flowing, dark auburn hair was always perfectly coiffed. My caramel skin was blemish free, and I always received compliments on my chestnut brown, almond eyes. I knew I was an exotic beauty and so did Warren.

"You don't look so bad yourself," I joked. He wasn't that cute in the face, but he was damn sure a clean-ass nigga when it came to putting his wears together. Warren and I had a laugh as we climbed into his champagne-colored Suburban.

The truck was just one of his many new toys. I was nervous, but I masked it behind my shades. We drove for a few minutes in silence.

Before I knew it, we were heading onto the highway. I guess Warren could feel my nerves in the air.

"It's all good, G-money. Everything gon' be a'ight, baby girl. I bet you that. We on our way to making it out of the game and way the fuck away from the hood. That's my word," Warren had said. Not even ten minutes had passed since the words had left his mouth. It seemed like as soon as we got on the highway with those fucking guns in the car, I saw the flashing lights behind us. I almost died of a heart attack.

"Oh, my God, Warren! Are they pulling us over?!" I exclaimed as I saw more and more cars with blue and red flashing lights coming out of the woodwork and surrounding us. My head whipped from side to side. Full-on panic set in on me and I swear I felt a little bit of piss leak out of my bladder. Me looking pretty in the front seat of the car like Warren had suggested didn't deter the Jake from pulling us over one bit like Warren had thought it would.

"Fuck!" Warren hissed. It took him a few minutes before he stopped the car. I guess he saw the look of terror on my face and decided not to try to outrun the cops. Besides, there would've been nowhere for him to run. There had to be at least ten black unmarked police vehicles surrounding us within no time.

"Warren, what is happening?! Oh, my God . . . you promised!" I screamed as my door was yanked open.

"That fucking Ant must've set me up! I'm sorry,

G-money!" was the last thing Warren said to me before he had also been yanked out of the vehicle and thrown to the ground facedown. The entire scene was surreal. I felt like I was in a bad dream. Those fucking pigs had no sympathy or mercy for me. They didn't care that I was in a dress, heels, or anything. I was thrown to the ground on my stomach just the same as if I were a fucking dude. My dress had blown up around my waist and all of my ass was on display. All I had on was a thong. I couldn't even pull my dress down because these bastards had my hands pulled behind my back in cuffs.

"Nice ass," one of those bastards said as I lay flat on my stomach completely fucking humiliated by all of their gawking eyes. Not to mention the eyes of all the cars that passed. There was so much rubbernecking so nosey people could see us on display out there. I was so mad at Warren for putting me in that position. What would my mother think of her only child going to jail for trafficking guns?! That was the only thought that ran through my mind. With my face planted in the dirt, I had immediately noticed that it wasn't just any routine police stop. I had heard enough hood legend stories to know this was the feds who had knocked us, especially judging from all the acronyms I read on the backs of their dark raid jackets—FBI, ATF, and DEA, to name a few.

"G-money! Don't tell them shit! Don't let them try to trick you!" Warren had yelled at me as he was roughly hoisted up from the ground and thrown in the back of another black vehicle.

I didn't want to hear shit from him right then. In fact, I

wanted to punch him in the fucking face for lying to me. The nerve of him to say this now! He had put my whole fucking life at risk. Warren had promised me that it would all be fine. He was so fucking sure that me being in the car would serve a greater good. I let that money and that good dick seduce me into being a straight-up dumb bitch to fall for that bullshit. I should have trusted my first instinct that told me, *Hell no, that shit is just a dumbass theory.*

I bit down into my bottom lip and tasted the dirt from the ground. That was where my life was at the moment—in the fucking dirt. I was sure Warren had money to pay lawyers, but me, little old Gianna Baker, girl from the hood who depended totally on her dude, didn't have shit. I realized then that everything I had on, all of the name-brand clothes, bags, shoes, where I lived, what I ate every day, all depended on Warren. I didn't have one red penny of my own saved. Even my fate now in this situation would depend on him. All I could do was cry just thinking about the entire situation. I knew my mother definitely didn't have shit herself. Shit, she was living off of me and Warren since I had been dating him. The situation was more grave than I could've ever imagined when Warren had asked me to do it.

Finally, it was my turn to be moved. I was never happier to be picked up out of the dirt. I was grabbed up off the ground roughly. At least one of the females on the scene did have the decency to pull my dress down. She couldn't save me from being roughly thrown into a vehicle with handcuffs digging into my wrists, though. As they were about to close the door of the car I was put in, I heard one of the feds yell out, "We found them! We found all of them!" I just closed my eyes at that point. I knew they had found the guns. I could've never imagined what kind of guns they were or how serious this shit really was until I heard them again. "Oh, and bonus! There are drugs in here too! These motherfuckers are going to burn."

Those words were like someone taking a dagger to my heart. Warren had lied to me. He had promised me that it would be all right, but he betrayed me. As if the guns weren't bad enough, Warren had drugs in the car too. I felt physically and mentally exhausted as those pigs drove me away from the scene in their spooky black unmarked car. They talked much shit for the entire ride. They were saying things like, "I guess your boyfriend threw you to the wolves," and "Well, take in as much of this daylight as you can, because you might not ever see the light of day again." I knew they were just trying to shake my resolve, and trust me, that shit was working like a charm.

4

What's Gonna Happen Next?

I didn't see Warren in person anymore after he'd been shoved into the other unmarked car. After a long car ride filled with jeers and taunts from the feds, I was whisked into a nondescript brick building, escorted onto an elevator that stopped on the tenth floor, and led down a long, scary hallway. At the end of the long hallway were several silver steel doors. The two agents who were handling me used a ring of keys to open one of the doors. My heart was hammering as I was placed in a drab room with gray walls, one steel table, and two steel chairs. The room smelled like stale bread and disinfectant. The scent immediately settled at the back of my throat and threatened to make me hurl. Warren and I were separated into different parts of the building. I knew this because I asked for him and that was the answer I had been given.

Before I knew it, hours had passed. Of course, I had no sense of the time. The only way I knew it had been hours was because my stomach was growling like a motherfucker.

During my time in that tiny, claustrophobic-ass room, those fucking feds had raked me over the coals. They finally had me to the point where I had broken. I was hungry, I had a headache, and I was scared. Not to mention I was confused and I just wanted to go the fuck home. I could fully understand how and why people gave false confessions just to get out of those severe interrogations. After I had been there for what seemed like forever, the snakes had started telling me that Warren was turning on me.

"He is singing like a bird. . . . He is blaming you for everything. . . . He is ready to make a deal that would put this all on you." Their words were swirling around in my head like the center of the Bermuda Triangle. I couldn't tell what was truth or fiction. The starvation had my brain on slow motion and I couldn't think. Still, I held my resolve.

"I don't fucking believe that. Warren would never do that to me," I'd hissed at them. They wouldn't relent. Then came the fucking icing on the cake. I could never forget when a fat, white agent with a Kojak shiny-ass bald head came into the room I was in. He held something in his hand. I eyed him suspiciously as he bent down and whispered something into the ear of the male agent who had been interrogating me. They both looked at me. Their expressions were stony.

"We have something we want you to see, Gianna. We want you to know the truth . . . we have no reason to lie to you," the bald guy said, his tone was like he was about to announce a death. He set the old clunky laptop he'd been holding down in front of me. No one said a word. He set up the screen, pressed a button, and Warren's face came into focus right before my eyes. "I'm telling you . . . she asked me to take her to meet a friend. I had no idea what was in the car," Warren was saying. I felt a sharp pain in my chest like someone had stuck their hand inside my chest and was squeezing my heart. I was blinking rapidly, that much I could tell. "She's a chick I was sleeping with, man. It wasn't like that between us at all. She was messing with some other dude who ran guns, but the sex was good so I kept messing with her," Warren said. I couldn't believe my fucking eyes. In fact, I didn't believe my eyes because the camera seemed to be fuzzy and his voice was different. Warren had denied that he knew about the fucking guns at all and blamed all that shit on me. It couldn't be real. It had to be some trickery on the part of those feds. But what the fuck did I know at that time? I was so flabbergasted after watching the video, I had thrown up right on the floor of the interrogation room. "See, Gianna. You better start talking and try to save yourself."

Finally, I told them I was ready to talk. But when the time really came for me to give my official statement, I had been scared to death and apprehensive. I was having second thoughts like a motherfucker. Snitching was a cardinal sin.

"Sign here," the Casper-the-friendly-ghost-looking ATF agent had said as he slid some paperwork in front of me. I squinted my eyes into little dashes and pursed my lips evilly at him. I was going through another bout of flip-flopping feelings. One minute I felt like the feds were on my side and trying to help me. The next minute, I felt like they were trying to set me up and get me to snitch on my man. The pale, white ATF agent in front of me had acted like a cocky piece of shit the whole time I had been there. I didn't like him. I rolled my eyes at him and folded my arms defiantly. I wasn't doing shit for him. My mind had changed so many times I didn't know if I was coming or going. Even if the video of Warren was real, that still didn't mean I had to stoop as low as he did and tell them pigs shit.

"Well, you agreed to give us the statement, didn't you? You have to give it to us in writing. We have to make sure what you tell us is true and that we can find you when it's time for you to testify against your little thug boyfriend," the agent continued, sliding the paperwork even closer to me. I wanted to jump up and slap the shit out of him. I was a complete emotional wreck. I felt stinky and dirty. I had hardly anything to eat but the chips and soda they'd finally given me. It was bad enough they had pulled us from Warren's car like we were fucking terrorists, now they had me trapped in a fucking room with really no fucking choice but to give them what they wanted. I closed my eyes and rocked back and forth. I was really caught up. I hated Warren so much at that moment. He had never loved me at all is what was racing through my mind. I put my head down on the table. My entire skull ached. The pain I felt in my head was worse than a migraine. I just really wanted to go home to my mother at that point.

"I know it's not easy to turn in your boyfriend, Gianna, but trust me . . . woman-to-woman. I've seen hundreds of girls get stiff sentences refusing to tell on their men. But, let me just tell you, while those poor girls do ten or more years in a federal penitentiary, their so-called men, who they sacrificed their freedom for, move on to the next chick and live happily ever after," the female ATF agent chimed in, moving so that she was sitting right next to me. I lifted my head up and looked at her. She was making sense. Her voice was also soft and comforting. More comforting than that fucking white prick partner of hers. The female agent wore a sympathetic look on her face. She was a black chick, fairly young, and surprisingly I felt a little sense of trust toward her. She placed her hand on my shoulder like a mother would her own child. Tears immediately started running down my face. This was some real bullshit I was in.

"I know it hurts, but think about the fact that he put you in this position in the first place. If what you told us so far was true about how you got into this mess. What man would risk his woman's freedom for guns? A woman he was supposed to love so much. That's not love, Gianna. Trust me, I wouldn't steer you wrong. As a woman, you have to look out for yourself in this situation. Just being in that car you are being considered as an accessory to some serious gun-trafficking charges. Not to mention the amount of drugs that were in the car. You could be facing some real hard time in a federal prison, very far away from your family," the female agent said, her tone soft and endearing. She was laying it on thick, though. I thought I could actually see the judge banging the gavel, sealing my fate. I put my hands on my head and grabbed handfuls of my hair between my fingers. I just wanted to scream and pull every strand of hair from my head. It was too much to think about. If Warren was in front of me right then, I knew I could have actually clawed his eyeballs out with my bare hands. I hated him! I had started to really think about what she was telling me. It's not like I had not heard of chicks in the hood getting the criminal justice book thrown at them, doing mad time, while I witnessed their dudes shitting on them in the streets. Some of them had even given birth behind bars, and those bastard ass niggas wouldn't even take the babies after the girls gave birth. Thinking about that made me shake my head, but I was still hesitant about cooperating. I felt like the only Sammy the Bull right then.

"Think about it, Gianna. Think about your own future. Think about how he used you. Don't think about Warren the so-called boyfriend who lied to you and told you he loved you; think about Warren the drug and gun dealer. You better seriously put yourself first in this situation, because trust me, sweetheart, he is over there singing like a blue jay and he ain't singing the let Gianna go free song," she'd said with feeling. I believed at that moment that she was really looking out for me. I had never considered that she was just trying to get her case against Warren. I lowered my eyes thinking about the decision I had to make to give a full written statement against Warren. It fucking wasn't easy. My stomach had started cramping and all. Basically, I had to decide whether I was going to snitch on my man to save my own ass or take a chance with him letting me take the fall. Although I was so in love at the time that I didn't think Warren would leave me for dead like that, I couldn't be sure, judging by how many bitches had been calling me on a daily basis saying they were with Warren. All kinds of shit started popping up to the surface of my mind. I guess you could say I didn't really trust him that much, not enough to put my own freedom on the line. I was so fucking mad at Warren for even putting me in that position. I mean, he had always been smarter than that. Finally, I threw my hands up in surrender.

"Here . . . just sign the agreement, Gianna. I wouldn't let you do anything that wasn't in your best interest. Us females have to stick together," the female agent pressed when she saw me starting to look a little bit like I'd turn Warren in. She continued to wear that soft look on her face like she truly sympathized with me. I was torn, but I also wanted to go home. I thought about how it would have killed my mother to find out that I was behind bars. Finally, I had decided it was Warren or me, bottom line. I picked up the black pen and signed every page of that fucking confidential informant paperwork. I felt much lighter as I did it too. I guess securing my own freedom had a way of taking a weight off of a person. I had sat there and told those fucking feds as much as I thought I knew about Warren's business . . . which admittedly wasn't much. I had even made some shit up just so I could get released faster. I figured the sweeter I made my cooperation seem, the faster I'd get the fuck out.

It had worked. I was brought before a federal magistrate judge the next day and released like nothing had ever happened. I had run from that fucking courthouse so fast it wasn't funny. I made it back to the apartment I shared with Warren and I gathered as much shit as I could. I wasn't stupid enough to believe I could continue living there without eventually feeling heat from Warren's people in the street. I was sure niggas would figure out real fast that I got out too fast. My initial intention was to take the ten or twenty thousand that I knew Warren always kept stashed in shoeboxes in his closet, but as I searched his shit, I found the little black velvet bag. It was like finding a pot of gold at the end of a rainbow. I remember how much more my heart rate had sped up as I dumped the content of the bag into my hand. My eyes were wide like marbles as I examined the bounty.

"This muthafucka!" I had gasped as I examined the huge, beautiful, crystal-clear diamonds one by one. I had counted out twenty diamonds. They were absolutely beautiful—clear, gleaming, and flawless. "These have to be worth some fucking cake!" I had murmured to myself.

I had to sit down for a minute after finding the diamonds. Warren was into more shit than I could've ever imagined. Judging from those fucking diamonds, he had also been holding out on much more money than I would have ever known about too. It didn't take long for me to decide to do what I did. At that moment, something had clicked inside of me. It was like a fight-or-flight instinct set me into motion. With those precious stones I knew I didn't need to take any of my many shoes, clothes, and handbags with me. That stuff would've just weighed me down, I had reasoned. I could buy all new belongings once I had found some place that would take the diamonds off my hands. I was scared to death leaving that house with those diamonds, but there had been no looking back once I made it outside. Honestly, my initial plan was to just sell a few and keep most of them so that I could return them to Warren whenever he came home. Okay, let me stop lying. I never intended to give Warren back shit. But I really didn't want to sell as many as I did as fast as I did. I had planned to make a new life with the stones.

Unfortunately, shit just seemed to spiral out of control. I had ended up taking the diamonds, Warren's 9mm Glock, and the ten thousand in cash he had in the house. I left DC in the thick of the night without telling my mother at first. I knew I'd eventually go back for her, though. When I first split, I stayed in touch with her using only throwaway phones. I told her that after the close call with the arrest, I needed to get out of town for a mental break. She bought the story, which I knew she would. I had finally gotten myself into a position that I could have my mother relocated. That's when I settled on Virginia Beach as a good place to settle down. I figured it was far enough from DC, but not so far that I'd be living in the boondocks somewhere.

The almost $250,000 I had made from selling the diamonds on the black market was gone in less than two years. After that, I was back to looking for a nigga to carry me. I guess you can say having a man take care of me was just how I was raised. The way I found Sidney was like magic. No lie, it seemed like everywhere I'd gone for a couple of weeks, I kept running into him. It was like fate kept bringing us into each other's path. Either that or he was following me. The way Sidney said it was that he'd been looking for me all of his life.

5

Preparing for the Worst

My cell phone rang and jolted me out of my daydream of the past. I could actually feel moisture between my legs from when I was thinking about having sex with Warren, but that couldn't even take away the overwhelming fear I felt in the pit of my stomach knowing that he was going to be on the streets soon. I knew better than anyone what Warren was capable of. I tried to shake off the thoughts as my ringing phone continued to distract me. I looked at the phone and saw that it was Sidney. A pang of nervousness hit me hard. I had been so lost in my own thoughts, I'd forgotten about meeting with Sidney for lunch.

"Shit! He must've been expecting me an hour ago," I said to myself out loud. I didn't even realize how long I had been sitting parked after my mother dropped that fucking bomb on me. I inhaled and exhaled before I picked up the phone. I noticed right away how terribly my hands were shaking. I was going to have to get myself together. There was no way

I could show up in front of Sidney coming apart mentally like this.

"Hey, baby," I answered with the phoniest cheer in my voice. "No. No . . . I'm okay. Yes, I'm still coming to see you. There was an accident . . . yeah, you know how that is. Lots of traffic out here. But I'm out of the worst of it now. I'll be there in a few," I fabricated on the spot. I could hear the shakiness in my own voice and wondered if Sidney could tell as well. I got off the phone as quickly as I could. It was a damn good thing Sidney was an older man, who was secure and not the type who sweated my every move. A younger street dude might've asked way more questions about why I'd been so late before so readily taking my word for it.

"Okay, Gigi. Get your shit together and go see your man. You can deal with what's to come later," I pep talked myself as I pulled my car back onto the road. I couldn't help finding myself lost deep in thought about what might come of Warren knowing that I had run my ass from DC to Virginia. I also thought about my life in DC and my new life in Virginia. The differences were very clear to me.

I must admit, when I first met Sidney, I wasn't all that attracted to him. My first impression at a glance was that he was an old man trying to get his swerve on with a younger woman to recapture his youth. He was already balding and graying, even in his beard. I have to say, though, he was well dressed in the older man sense. He was smooth enough with his approach, too; but what really caught my eye was the Presidential Rolex gleaming from Sidney's wrist. I was all eyes and ears once I saw that. His very pregnant wallet was also something I remember being an eye-catcher to me at that time. Sidney was more low key than I ever remember Warren being, and that made me say maybe I should give this man a try.

I did and it led us to marriage really fast. We didn't date much at all. Sidney asked me to marry him and said something like, "I'm supposed to watch over you til death do us part . . . be my wife." I had been so hard up for money after burning up all my money that he could've said anything and I would've probably said yes at that time. Married, nice life, and all of the luxury things I wanted. The fact still remained that when I did the comparison of my men, you would know that Sidney could never compare to Warren in certain areas and vice versa. One was young, all about that street life, and could lay the pipe like a fucking expert. The other was older, all about building a real wealthy lifestyle, and was less than amusing in the bed. But he made up for it with how he gave me everything in the world. If I had to stand them side by side, there would be drastic differences that made each of them invaluable in their own right. Warren was thirty-three years old, stood six feet three inches, had six-pack abs, round, deep-set eyes, and deep chocolate skin. Warren dressed like a street dude, donning the latest premium denim and high-end sneakers that hit the stores before anyone else in the hood could even dream about it. Sidney, on the other hand, was forty-five years old, stood a mere five feet nine inches, had a small, protruding gut, high yellow skin, salt and pepper hair, and little beady eyes that weren't readily attractive. Sidney was older, more distinguished, and he dressed like it.

He always wore dress pants; albeit tailor-made, they were still dress pants. He preferred Ferragamo loafers and hard-bottom gators over any other footwear. French cuff shirts were the order of the day whenever Sidney went out to conduct business. Just like there were definitely stark differences between the two men, so was the life I had had with each.

When I was with Warren, I was always on edge about other bitches. Warren had cheated a few times to say the least. I also never knew if I would get a call saying he was dead or had been arrested for some shit, so whenever he was in the streets and my cell phone rang, it sent a sense of dread through me. Life with Warren was always an adventure. I never knew what any given day would hold whether it was shopping trips, wild parties, or a day of straight animalistic sex from sunup until sundown. Most of the things Warren bought me were hood rich shit, like Gucci bags, the latest True Religion or Seven for All Mankind jeans, and shit that chicks in the hood saved up their pennies to get. Warren had brought me up from the streets, so for a while I felt a sense of loyalty toward him. Life with Sidney was routine, predictable, and some days even mundane. He went to run his businesses or on business trips and I played the role of kept woman. I didn't ever have to worry about another woman calling me. My cell phone rang at the same time every day with the same call from Sidney. I tried to do spontaneous things like the lunch surprise today, but I knew it kind of made Sidney uncomfortable. Sex with him was blah, mundane. I always tried to spice it up, but as long as I couldn't buy him a new dick, it would still be the same. Sidney's wealth allowed me to shop for things I'm sure girls from my old neighborhood had never experienced. When I got with him, it was all Akris, Celine, and Hermes bags, clothes from Thakoon, Diane Von Fürstenberg, and shoes from Christian Louboutin and 3.1 Phillip Lim. Grown folks shit. After getting with Sidney, I also had the pleasure of having my name added to those special black lists in all of the designer shops. Those snooty-ass stores would've never allowed Warren to add his name to those lists no matter how much drug and gun money that nigga had.

Sidney was eighteen years older than me, which my mother hated right away. "He has already lived his life, Gianna. He will stop you from living yours. Men like him just want a trophy wife," my mother had preached behind Sidney's back after she'd first met him. Sidney's family apparently felt the same way about me. He had five kids who all hated me. Those fucking brats made my life hell when they were around. I was only four years older than his eldest daughter, Arianna, which caused lots of problems with the kids and his ex-wives. And forget about Sidney's crotchety-ass mother. That old bitch hated me with a passion. She was constantly telling Sidney that I was no good for him; that I was just using him for his money; and that before she died she would see to it that our marriage ended. I had many run-ins with his mother . . . none of them positive. I once heard his mother on speakerphone call me a scam artist and a fucking gold digger. Sidney loved me, that much I felt like I knew for sure. He never let his family come in between us. I cared about him and maybe I even love him by now, but I wasn't in love with Sidney like

I had been with Warren. Those were feelings I could never get over, but I'd tried like hell to put those shits to the far reaches of my mind. I thought running away and never seeing Warren again would cause the feelings to all die, but now I know better. All it took was a mention of him to dredge them all back up to the surface.

6

My Mission

When my Range Rover pulled into the Costner Luxury Cars parking lot, I immediately noticed that Sidney was in front of the door with his arms folded. I could tell he had been waiting on me, because as owner of the lot, he hardly ever stood outside.

"Here we go. Get ready for it," I mumbled to myself. I got my nerves together, plastered on a fake smile, and climbed out of the vehicle. "Hi, baby. What are you doing out here?" I sang real phony-like. I came around and opened the passenger door so I could retrieve the soul food I had bought for our little lunch date.

Sidney didn't answer my question. Not a good sign. He approached just as I used my hip to close the door. His face was serious. I could tell there were going to be more questions coming from his ass. I wasn't really in the mood for the third degree. My mind was all over the place. I felt a buzz of annoyance flitting through me. I didn't want to take it out on Sidney. It wasn't his fault that my entire world had come crashing down on me today.

"That was a long time," Sidney said, his naturally deep voice making my insides churn. I closed my eyes for a few seconds trying to get my mood together. I wish he would stop fucking with me right now. I kept smiling and singing. It was all I could do to keep my nerves and my anger at bay. I didn't want to take it out on him.

"Yeah, that traffic was a bitch," I replied, avoiding eye contact. Sidney could always tell when something was wrong with me by the look on my face. Call it "older man intuition" or whatever, but he was a very good read of people's expressions. He was watching me closely; I could feel the heat of his gaze on me. I tried to quickly get the heat off of me.

"C'mon, let's go inside so we can finally have our little lunch date, honey," I said sweetly, trying to hurry up and get past the subject about the reason for my being so late. Sidney let out a long sigh, which caused my heart to speed up. Can he tell I'm lying? Why doesn't he just leave the subject alone! I screamed inside my head. I really didn't need the aggravation right now.

"I'm sorry, Gigi, but I won't be able to eat with you. I have a very big client coming in a few minutes," Sidney said, his words coming out of his mouth in rapid succession. I stopped walking. My feelings quickly changed from annoyed nervousness to straight annoyance.

"Why didn't you tell me that shit over the phone?!" I snapped, turning this situation around to put him on the defensive. Maybe I could get him to forget about how I kept him waiting. "Why would you let me ride all the way here, deal with that traffic, if you knew you had a client coming?" I asked, raising my voice.

"No . . . no, baby, listen. This appointment was made after I spoke with you earlier. The client says he heard about me and wants to deal only with me. Says a good friend of his recommended me for what I can do for him," Sidney said in a low whisper. The words made cramps rumble through my stomach. Another exclusive client deal, that's what got Warren and me into the bullshit we got into back then. I shuddered at the thought. Warren would not stop running through my damn head now.

Sidney stepped closer to me. "C'mon, Gigi, I'm truly sorry, but you know how I make most of my money here with this recession, don't you? How I keep you in all those fine clothes and that big-ass house . . ." Sidney whispered, his tone kind of chastising.

I exhaled. I knew he was referring to the fact that ninety percent of his customers were drug dealers who paid him with cash so they could get the hottest new whips on the road. Sidney worked up the paperwork for them so that they could buy cars without the hassle of all the explanations you have to go through at the legitimate dealerships. All the hustlers in Virginia Beach knew that Sidney was the one who could put them behind the wheel of their dream car and there would be no questions asked. It would cost them much more for the car, but what the hell did they care when their money was all dirty anyway. Of course, Sidney got his cut out of the deals. A big cut, I might add. Which, in turn, benefitted me; so who was I to really complain. Yet, I was feeling stressed and devilish, so I wasn't going to relent that easily.

"Yes, I know all about how you make your money since you keep reminding me how you work so hard to keep me," I answered, rolling my eyes. I hated when he made me feel like I was a moocher or some shit. Sidney liked to hold his financial support over my head whenever he got the chance. Most of the time I didn't care because I felt like, as his wife, I deserved everything I got. Shit, I was fucking his old ass almost every night, and trust me, his dick game was nowhere near Warren's. Most times I had to do lots of mental preparation to fuck Sidney.

"Don't be like that, Gigi. I do this all for us. Just understand that I can't let this deal . . ." Sidney was saying. Suddenly, I couldn't hear him anymore. My ears were literally fucking ringing. As he kept rambling I could see his mouth moving, but I couldn't hear him because I had noticed a familiar figure heading straight toward us. I would recognize that walk anywhere. I swear I felt like someone had reached into my chest and clamped down on my heart with a vise grip. My eyes widened as big as dinner plates. My breath was caught in my throat. I stared out of the large glass window of the dealership, my feet seemingly rooted to the floor. I could not stop staring as the threat got closer and closer and came more into focus. Sidney noticed my gaze and looked out the window too. Sidney smiled. I wasn't fucking smiling at all. My mind was telling me to run, but some unknown force was holding me still. Goose bumps rose on my arms and legs. Sidney was as cheery as a fucking Cheshire cat.

"Oh . . . there he is. That client I was telling you about. That's got to be him. He said he'd be wearing a red shirt," Sidney said excitedly.

What the fuck! I can't believe this shit! Run, Gigi! Run!! my mind was telling me.

"Tha . . . that's . . . um . . . your client," I stuttered, totally stunned. I didn't even realize I had dropped the bags of food at my feet. I think my mouth was even hanging open.

"Gigi . . . what is it?" Sidney asked, looking from me to the window and back again. He must've been thinking I was straight-up crazy.

"Um . . . I have to use the ladies' room," I said nervously. Before I knew it my legs were in motion. My brain had finally told my stupid ass to get the fuck out of dodge before that so-called client made it to where Sidney and I stood. I almost broke into a full-out sprint just as I heard the chimes on the dealership door ring indicating someone had entered. I raced into the bathroom and pushed my way inside of the last empty stall. I slammed the door behind me and slid the lock to secure the door. My chest was heaving up and down, and sweat had literally broke out on my entire body. My lips felt chapped from having my mouth open breathing so hard. Good thing I was in a bathroom already because I sure felt like I would shit, piss, and throw up all at the same time.

I rested my back against the stall door and stared straight at the wall. I could see Warren's scowling face very clearly in my mind's eye now. He was coming for my ass, that was for sure. There wasn't shit I could do about it. I literally felt like I was having a heart attack. I placed my hand on my chest, trying to will myself to calm down.

"Oh, my God! He is going to kill me for what I did," I gasped. I couldn't move, completely paralyzed with fear. Tears stung at the backs of my eyes as I thought about what was happening right now. I had done some foul shit, but I thought for sure I could put it all behind me. I guess not. A part of my past was standing right in the same building with me, probably shaking hands with my poor unsuspecting husband. The thought of Sidney being in harm's way made me hunch over and gag. I dry heaved several times, but I couldn't vomit.

Sidney was right outside of the door conducting business with Ace—Warren's right-hand man and best friend since childhood. I knew for sure Warren had definitely sent Ace to the dealership after he found out from my stupid-ass mother that I was married to Sidney Costner. That had to be the explanation for Ace showing up. There wasn't that much fucking coincidence in the world! Ace was a straight DC dude; no way he needed to come all the way to Virginia to cop a whip from my husband. I hadn't seen Ace since days before I had done what I did to Warren. Ace had been right in the courtroom when Warren was sentenced. Fortunately, I had made it out of the building before Ace had had the chance to confront me. I'd known Ace for all of the years I had been with Warren, and I knew that Ace was more ruthless and dangerous than Warren could ever be. I heard Ace was the one who executed Ant after all of the speculation that the feds came down on Warren and me that day too easily. The streets had been reporting that Ant hadn't actually gotten into a DV situation with his baby mother. Instead, he had actually been at the police station setting Warren up. Well, needless to say, Ant was found with half of his head missing from a gunshot blast he took in the back of it. Ace was said to be the executioner.

Paranoia had fully taken over as I stood cowering in the bathroom. I jumped when I heard the bathroom door open. I could barely control my breathing. I just knew Ace had already shot Sidney and was coming into the bathroom to get me now. I bit down hard into my bottom lip as I quietly moved toward the toilet, slid my heels off, and climbed atop the toilet seat so Ace couldn't see my feet under the stall door. My legs shook uncontrollably and burned like hell as I crouched with my knees bent. Sweat dripped from my forehead into my eyes, but I didn't dare move to wipe it away. I listened to the footsteps on the tile floor. I said a silent prayer for my soul and for my mother. I knew she would just die when she found out I'd been shot down like a dog execution style in a fucking bathroom stall. I swallowed hard as the footsteps stopped. It seemed like an eternity before I finally heard the toilet a few stalls away flush. The sound from the toilet flushing almost made me throw up with nervousness. Maybe that's just a ploy to get me to blow my hiding spot. Maybe Ace wants me to think it's just someone using the toilet and when I climb down from here, he will get me. All kinds of thoughts ran through my mind. But then I realized Ace wasn't the hide-the-ball type of nigga. If he was going to come in and shoot my ass, it would've been a wrap already. Finally, I heard the main bathroom door open again and then there was silence. Whoever it was had just used the toilet and left. The bitch hadn't even washed her nasty-ass hands. Whew! I breathed a sigh of relief. I guess it hadn't been Ace trying to kill me after all. I let out a long, exasperated breath as I climbed down off the toilet. I shook my head from side to side trying to get my thoughts back in order. I slid back into my heels and carefully opened the stall lock. I peeked out. The bathroom was empty except for me.

"Stop it, Gianna. You're being stupid now. Warren wouldn't be able to find you and send Ace that quickly. Maybe it was just a coincidence that he was at Sidney's dealership," I mumbled to myself. Convincing myself that this was all just some crazy fluke was going to be the only way I could mentally deal with it right now. I walked over to the sinks and splashed water onto my face. I looked as pale as a ghost, not my usual glowing caramel complexion. My long, auburn hair was frazzled as shit from the sweat. I had to stop being crazy. I smoothed my clothes out and opened the bathroom door. I can't lie; I was still scared as shit. My thick, muscular legs did me no good right now because they were shaky as shit when I walked out of the door.

I moved slowly and carefully. Strangely, the dealership was like a ghost town. I crinkled my eyebrows as I looked around at the unusually quiet space. There were empty desks and all of the salespeople seemed to have just disappeared. This caused an uneasy feeling to come over me. Are they all dead? Did Ace herd everybody into a room and start shooting them, looking for me? How many times do all of the salespeople have clients at the same time . . . not very often. I also didn't see Sidney or Ace and trust me, I was looking for them. *Fuck it! Just make a run for it, Gigi,* I finally told myself. I was praying I could make it to my car and out of there before anyone could see me. I started moving faster toward the door, but my effort was short-lived.

"Well, well, well," I heard the unmistakable raspy voice coming from my left. My heart dropped into my stomach and I froze. "Gigi the snitch. Or should I say the snitch and the thief," the voice said.

My head whipped around frantically and I finally saw Ace walking toward me. I could've turned into a pile of salt right then and there. My nerves were completely unhinged, but I had no choice but to play it cool. My nostrils flared like a bull's.

"Not here, Ace," I whispered harshly. Surprisingly, the adrenaline rushing through my veins had given me a big boost of courage that had shocked even me. I tried to keep walking.

Ace was on me within a second. He grabbed my arm roughly. "Don't worry . . . your old man is busy working numbers in the office, so he won't see us. And I made sure I brought enough goons with me to keep those fucking sales guys busy too. Oh, yeah, and the secretary is in there helping your hubby crunch the numbers . . . it's all taken care of, G-money. All planned out just like this visit to Virginia," Ace said through clenched teeth as he painfully tightened his grip on my arm. Hearing Ace say Warren's nickname for me made me want to cry. I wasn't about to show fear, though. I had to play hardball or else Ace would know I was scared shitless. I tried to wrestle my arm away from him, but that just made him clamp down harder. Pain shot up my arm.

"Yeah, but other people will see right in through those glass windows and there are loads of surveillance cameras around here. So go ahead and do something stupid. Your ass will be hemmed the fuck up so fast," I whispered.

Ace smiled like I had won. He finally let me go. "You're right. This is not the time or place to discuss the seriousness of the shit you're in. You need to meet me tonight in Norfolk at nine-thirty sharp. We got some big shit to discuss. You know I mean business because your real husband sent me. He is not going to rest on this one, Gigi," Ace whispered back, a serious expression spreading over his face. I felt like shitting on myself right then and there.

"I will meet you," I answered roughly. I started to walk away but was startled to hear Sidney so close.

"You know Mr. Ace?" Sidney's voice came from behind me. My knees actually felt weak; Ace looked surprised too. Neither one of us knew just how much of our exchange Sidney had seen and overheard. It was like he had just materialized out of the walls.

"Oh, nah, nah, Mr. Costner. I thought your wife was this no-good chick who I knew from DC, but it's not her," Ace answered Sidney's question, wearing a sinister grin. Ace was being a smartass. Sidney looked from Ace to me and back again. I had a silly, nervous grin on my face. I couldn't even say a word. All of the words were caught in my throat like I'd swallowed a handful of hard marbles.

"Sorry for the misunderstanding, miss," Ace said, smiling again.

"No . . . no . . . um . . . no problem," I replied with a nervous laugh. "Sidney, I will see you at home tonight," I said to my husband, turning on my heels. I hauled ass out of the dealership doors like somebody had set my ass on fire. I didn't even give Sidney a chance to answer me back. I was behind the wheel and screeching my tires out of the parking lot within a few minutes. My hands shook so badly I could hardly steer the car. I had to come up with a plan to deal with this situation. I knew exactly what Warren was after. I also knew he wasn't going to rest until he got what he was looking for.

7

Secrets and Lies

After my encounter with Ace, driving home had been a task, to say the least. Every car that passed me on the highway made me jump. Every horn made me feel like I'd have a heart attack from fright. I could not get home fast enough.

I pulled up to my estate and jumped out of my car, barely putting the vehicle in Park. I was moving so fast that my heels sounded like firecrackers popping against the tiled pathway as I rushed up to my front door. With trembling hands I fished my keys from my bag, but it took me a few damn tries to get into the house. Finally, I raced into the house with one fucking thing on my mind. I needed to move my stash, which I hadn't looked at in so long. I'd been so financially secure living off of Sidney that I hadn't even bothered to check on my little secret hidden treasure. I called it my rainy day insurance, but in light of what was going on now, I was going to have to do things differently. It was mine now, but the shit hadn't always belonged to me. My mind was focused on getting upstairs to my closet before Sidney came home. He didn't know anything about what I had done in my past and what I had hiding right under his nose. I was also scouring my brain to think of where I could move my stash. I considered going to the bank and getting a private safe deposit box, but there was record keeping involved with that shit. I needed something highly secretive. Just as I got inside I heard the house phone ringing.

"Fuck!" I huffed. I didn't need any distractions right now. I knew it was either Sidney or my nagging-ass mother. No one else called the house phone at all. I was too focused on my task at hand to answer it, so I ignored it. I barely made it up my spiral staircase that led to the bedrooms before the phone was ringing again. "Are you kidding me?" I grumbled. If I didn't answer it I knew both of them would just keep on calling back. I walked into my bedroom and picked up the cordless on the nightstand. I still couldn't figure out why we even had a house phone. Cell phones were all we ever used anyway. "Hello?!" I barked into the phone breathlessly.

"Damn . . . why you sound so mad?" the voice filtered through the receiver. All of the color drained from my face and I felt weak. They even had my house phone number, which certainly meant that not only did they know where Sidney worked, but they also knew exactly where we lived. I couldn't even speak at first.

"I called to remind you about our meeting tonight. I really like your old man, too . . . good ol' Mr. Sidney Costner. I wonder how he would feel knowing his little well-kept wife was a former hood rat, snitching-ass thief from the projects in DC?"

Ace said, his raspy voice making me cringe like hearing nails on a chalkboard.

"I hope you don't try no bullshit and you're there tonight," he continued. "Don't make me do anything horrible to your old man cuz that's what's gon' happen if you try not to show up," Ace said with evil finality. I was feeling a mixture of anger and fear. How dare that muthafucka call my house! The house I shared with my husband! They were crossing the fucking line now! I held the phone so tightly my knuckles turned white. My jaw rocked so feverishly I was giving myself a migraine.

"Are you there, Mrs. Costner?" Ace asked slyly.

"How did you get my number?" I whispered harshly. It was all I could come up with at that moment. Too many things were fighting a battle in my mind to say anything more sophisticated.

"How the fuck you think I got it! Bitch, we know everything. Including what you took from the house when you snitched on my crew and ran. We want what belongs to us, so be ready to fucking talk about that tonight," Ace boomed. I closed my eyes. I had a feeling those fucking diamonds would eventually come back to haunt me. I just didn't think it would be so soon.

"What do y'all want from me? I did what I had to do to save myself. If it was up to Warren I would've been left for dead!" I gritted. That was the truth. Warren would've been fine letting me take the fall for his bullshit.

"Yo . . . at this point, we don't even give a fuck that you ran your trap to the feds. All we want is what you took. You caused a war when you took that shit, and trust me we've been looking for you for a while now. It just took a while to get the information from your mother. My man Warren is on the hook for the shit you did and if you know like I know, you know that nigga ain't about to tell these dangerous muthafuckas that he got stuck up by no bitch. Especially his own bitch," Ace spat. I knew he was right too. Warren had a lot of pride, and he was all about upholding his street credibility by any means necessary.

"I don't know what you're talking about," I lied real quick. There would be no confessions coming from me. "All I did was tell the feds that those guns weren't mine. I never said they were Warren's. I guess they assumed the shits were Warren's. I never snitched and I ain't got shit that belongs to you or Warren. Now leave me the fuck alone!" I screamed. I wished that little bit of base in my voice had worked, but it didn't. Ace wasn't swayed one bit.

"Just be there tonight, bitch! Or else," Ace barked. Then he clicked the phone off.

I held it for a few seconds, thinking about the gravity of it all. Things were happening so fucking fast I felt like a hamster on a wheel.

"Agggh!" I screamed as I forcefully snatched the phone line out of the wall. I collapsed onto the floor, no longer able to stand. I was emotionally and physically spent from the happenings of the day. I knew this shit was serious and that it was just going to keep getting worse. I also knew I no longer had all of what Ace and Warren were looking for. There was no way for me to get them back either. I rushed into my huge walk-in closet and raced over to one of Sidney's safes. I struggled to move the heavy black metal safe, but after some effort I was finally able to get it moved from covering the spot on the floor I needed. I quickly lifted up the small, loose square of carpet that had been hidden under the safe. I used my long nails and peeled back the carpet to reveal the plywood floor underneath. I exhaled and used my nail to lift up a plank of the wood. Under the loosened plank was the small black velvet drawstring bag. I retrieved it, held it in my hand, and closed my eyes. My pulse still sped up whenever I held those diamonds. They had been like bad luck charms since the day I'd taken them. I clutched the small bag so tightly my hand hurt. I collapsed onto the floor and the tears just poured from my eyes. Up until that minute I had never regretted taking that tiny bag from Warren's house. I don't know what I was thinking that day I was trying to get the fuck out of dodge, but today I was full of regret for what I had done. Swallowing hard, I finally peered into the bag at the four remaining raw diamonds inside. The medium-sized gems twinkled even in the dimmest light. They were still beautiful. I had saved the remaining four as financial security in case shit with Sidney and I didn't work out, but those four diamonds were all that was left of the twenty I had stolen. Warren and Ace wouldn't be looking for just four diamonds . . . they'd be looking for twenty flawless raw uncut diamonds that were probably worth way more than the $250,000 I'd gotten rid of them for. I was so fucking stupid! I had certainly acted like a hood rat the way I ran through that money. Buying shoes, clothes, handbags, and paying to stay in high-priced hotels. I hadn't even been smart enough at the time to buy a piece of property for myself. Now I had nothing to show for it. I was living off of my husband, whom I cared about but didn't love. Again, depending on a man for everything. I had my mother depending on me and once again I was in deep shit with no way out but to throw someone under the fucking bus. But who would it be? Sidney? Stealing from him wasn't an option. He kept his shit under strict lock and key. I lay on the floor of a grand house that I lived in with my husband thinking about how shit had gone so wrong and what I was going to do to get myself out of this mess. I had learned after the dustup with Warren and the feds that I had to put myself first always. Somebody wasn't going to make it out of this shit alive. My mission was to make sure it wasn't me.

I heard Sidney calling my name from downstairs. I didn't even realize I had fallen asleep on the floor of the closet while daydreaming of my checkered past. I bolted upright at the sound of Sidney's voice.

"Fuck!" I whispered. I couldn't afford for him to come up there and find me with the safe moved away and my hiding spot for the diamonds exposed. I didn't want to put the diamonds back in the same place, but I had no time to think of another place.

"I'm coming down, Sidney!" I yelled back to stave him off for a few minutes. I knew how much his old ass hated coming up those stairs unless he was ready to go to bed, so I figured that would buy me some time. I raced around the closet, placing the diamonds back into the floor. I struggled to get the safe back over the spot. Just as I finished and stood up, I heard Sidney behind me.

"Gigi? Are you all right?" His voice was accusatory. Or maybe I was just so paranoid I heard it as being accusatory.

I almost jumped out of my fucking skin. He had definitely snuck up on me. I was panting after moving the safe back. My eyes were stretched wide with surprise. I had to place my hand over my chest to keep my heart from jumping loose of my chest bone.

"Sidney! Don't sneak up on me like that!" I boomed, still holding my chest in a clutch-the-pearl manner. Sidney's brows furrowed with confusion.

"What were you doing in the closet? You've been a little weird all day," Sidney made me aware of his observation. He also ignored my outbursts. He eyed me suspiciously and looked around the closet the same way. I immediately felt like a child being chastised. Anger welled up inside of me like a pot about to boil over.

"What are you talking about?! Why are you acting like I'm some child to be questioned? I tried to do something nice for you today! But excuse me for trying to be spontaneous in this boring-ass marriage of ours! I keep forgetting all you like is missionary sex and the same routine! You'd rather be with a fucking client than have lunch with me, and now you want to come in here accusing me of being weird!!" I exploded, pushing past him until I was out of the closet. I needed to get him to stop focusing on the inside of that damn closet. Sidney seemed dumbfounded by my sudden outburst. He whirled around on his heels and followed me with his eyes. I had even surprised myself. It was all part of the plan. I knew I had to start an argument with Sidney, so his questions just made it that much easier for me to pick a fight. How else would I get out of the house at night without questions?

"Gigi . . . um . . . I didn't mean it that way," Sidney said, apologetically putting his hands up in front of him. I swear he looked like I had just slapped him in the face. I felt badly, but I had to keep up the act.

"Yeah, you never mean shit when you treat me like I'm one of your kids. That's what the fuck I get fucking with a man who thinks he's my father. Please . . . just leave me alone. I'm going out!" I continued my tirade for good measure. I had to make it seemed as real as possible. I also had to make it all Sidney's fault so that whenever I returned home he wouldn't ask me any more fucking questions.

"Are you done with your inquisition?!" I asked, hand on my hip. Sidney just stared at me like I was crazy. "Good! And don't blow up my fucking cell phone while I am out. I'll be home whenever I get back here!" I boomed. I kind of felt bad once I was out of the house. I knew Sidney didn't deserve what I had just done. But it was either that or put him in harm's way. I left the house unaware of what would happen next. All I could do now was pray.

8

Payback Is a Bitch

Driving to the meeting place, I'd thought about calling my mother to tell her I loved her, just in case. I'd even picked up my cell phone several times and dialed her number only to hang it up. I finally thought it best not to worry her, because knowing my mother, she would've sent the police out to find me or, worse, called Sidney and had him out on the streets looking for me.

I slowed my car down near Highway 264. A sense of dread filled me as I looked out at the place I was going. There was nothing fucking pretty about it, that was for sure. Anything could happen there without anyone noticing for a long time. Ace had instructed me to meet him at the Tides stadium parking lot in Norfolk. Everyone knew that the stadium parking lot was under Highway 264, which was desolate as hell at night. It definitely was no place for me. Only drug fiends, rapists, and other scary-ass creeps hung out there after the sun went down. A fact that didn't give me a good feeling inside while heading to the stadium. I imagined a hundred things Ace might say or, worse, do to me when I arrived. Ace wasn't the nicest person in the world, that was a fact. It didn't matter if you were a woman or a man, if he wanted you dead, you'd be dead. I had heard stories about how Ace had killed one of his baby mothers for stealing from him. Rumor had it he'd shot her in the back of the head and put her dead body on her mother's doorstep. Ace then went to court, acted like he had no clue what happened to the girl, and fought for custody of his son. Crazy shit! Warren told me he always depended on Ace when there was a really dirty job to be done . . . like when they wanted to wipe someone completely out. No remains was how they referred to the types of hits Ace carried out on niggas. He'd wipe out the person's entire existence. The only thing that might save me was the fact that I believed or at least hoped that Warren did love me at one time. Then again, I'm guessing Ace had cared about his baby mother at a time before he executed her ass too. Damn, hindsight was surely twenty-twenty. If I could rewind time, I might've just left town broke as hell—no diamonds, no money. I sighed. I couldn't change what I had done, so now I was going to face the music. I said more than one silent prayer as I peered out of my windshield at the deserted area. It was no place for a woman at night.

My heart thumped painfully against my sternum as I pulled my car slowly into the stadium parking lot. I could see a lone black SUV off in the distance as I inched my car forward at a snail's pace. I just assumed it was Ace and about three or four goons waiting, since that's how he and Warren rolled most of the time.

"It's showtime, Gigi," I whispered out loud to myself. I

touched the 9mm Glock I had sitting between my thighs for assurance. I had already made up my mind that I was going to try and go out in a blaze of glory if they tried anything crazy. At least I would've been known to put a fight before my demise. I stopped my car a few feet away from the vehicle and I flicked my headlights from regular to high beam and back again. I wasn't about to just get out and leave myself wide open to be shot down like a dog, but at the same time, I wanted to let Ace know I was there and ready to hear what he had to say. There was no immediate reaction to my signal. That was strange. I waited a few minutes after flicking the lights and still didn't see any movement in the car. I flicked the lights again, this time I did it a few more times than I had the first time. Again, I waited. Still no movement. I let out a long sigh. I started to sweat so badly I felt the beads rolling down the center of my back.

"What the fuck, Ace?!" I whispered harshly. I was completely unnerved now. All that was visible in the distance around my car was darkness. I couldn't hear shit due to the cars whizzing by overhead. Ace was playing a game probably to see how fucking scared I was, and it was working. Or maybe he wanted to see if I was going to come with the police or something. I inhaled deeply and exhaled a windstorm. I fanned myself with my hands. "Calm down, Gigi. Calm down." I gave myself a pep talk to try and calm my nerves. It didn't work at all. My teeth were literally chattering.

I squinted my eyes again, but with my headlights shining straight on the SUV like a spotlight there was a horrible back glare and I could not see anyone inside the vehicle through the windshield. I finally thought to turn my lights off thinking without the glare I could see something. I quickly realized that the vehicle was empty inside. Plus, now the entire fucking place was pitch black without my lights. I crinkled my eyebrows, confused as an ominous feeling washed over me. My chest heaved as I quickly realized this was a fucking setup at its best. "What the fuck?!" I whispered as my hands shakily grabbed for the gear stick to put my car into Reverse. I was about to break out of there because I wasn't feeling the atmosphere at all. I was so scared I couldn't get my hands to calm down long enough to get to the gearshift. I didn't get the chance to move to change gears before I heard *BANG! BANG! BANG!* The sound had come from outside the car.

"Aggghh!!" I screamed, instinctively throwing my hands up over my ears, ducking in response to the loud noises. My ears were literally ringing within a matter of minutes. I knew right away it was gunshots I had heard. Before I could do anything else I felt the cool night air wisp into my car. I jumped fiercely. That's when I realized my driver's side door had been snatched open. I looked over quickly, but all I got the chance to see was a big black figure.

"Agghgh!" I screamed again when I felt the presence of someone near me. I could literally feel the person's breath on my face. My scream was short-lived. I felt big, powerful hands on my left arm and left leg. Then suddenly my head was being jerked and tugged too. I tried in vain to hold on to my seat, then the steering wheel, but my efforts were futile. Within minutes I was forcefully dragged from my car. I let out another half scream. I heard my handgun skitter to the ground. All hope of protecting myself was gone now. My screams were all for nothing because my mouth was covered by a big gorilla hand. Between the force and the fear, I could not catch my breath. I was hyperventilating. I just knew I was going into shock from being so scared. "Mmmm!" I moaned as I tried to move my head. That was futile too. I was being held like a ragdoll. I tried to scream for help, but my muffled words were barely audible. I knew whoever was holding me was probably powerful enough to snap my neck right there. My mind had drawn a complete blank. Suddenly, I felt a very thick, muscular arm closing around my neck. I gagged from being put in a chokehold. I tried to claw at the thick, meaty arm that was causing me to suffocate, but I could hardly muster enough strength to make any leeway. I immediately felt my air supply being cut off. My ears were still ringing from the gunshots, but I could still hear faint voices around me.

"Let's move this bitch before we have witnesses," one of them said; that much I could make out.

"Yeah, there's a little building over there. We can do what we gotta do in there," someone else said. They kept whispering about my fate. I knew I was going to die, but I wasn't going to go out without a struggle.

Fighting for my life, I tried to flail and kick. I actually tired myself out because I wasn't making any headway with the monsters that were holding me. All of that effort and I was no match for whoever was accosting me. I even thought I heard them laughing at my efforts. The more I scratched and clawed at the huge chunk of meaty arm around my neck, the tighter it got. Finally, I had been devoid of air for so long total blackness engulfed me. There was no fighting that dark cloud that closed in on me. I just knew I was a goner.

* * *

"G-money. G-money, I know you hear me . . . look at me."

I came into consciousness hearing Warren's nickname for me being called. My eyes fluttered to the sound, but I couldn't open them.

"Yo! Wake the fuck up!"

I was immediately aware of the sharp pains shooting through my head as I tried in vain to get my heavy eyelids to open. "Mmmm," I moaned as I became painfully aware of my surroundings. Suddenly I felt a sharp pain penetrate the side of my face. "Ugh," I grunted from the pain. I actually felt my jaw click from the hit. I didn't have enough energy to scream. I felt a more intense sensation on the other side of my face. I had been slapped on the other cheek this time.

"Wake the fuck up, bitch!" I heard a gruff voice boom. I finally forced my hyposensitized eyes open. There were at least five people in the room, that much I could tell as I counted the blurry shadows. Someone was walking toward me with fists clenched.

"Please," I rasped, flinching. My throat felt like someone had shoved a firelit pole down it. I was hit across the face again. This time the metallic taste of blood filled my mouth. Tears immediately sprang to my eyes. Not only did I think they were going to kill me, but it seemed like they were going to torture me first. "Please," I pleaded again through tears.

"Oh, now you want to say please," a familiar voice said to me as the person grabbed a handful of my hair and yanked my downturned head up so that my battered eyes met his gaze.

"Warren?" I murmured through my swollen lips. It was crystal clear now. I was staring in the devilish eyes of my ex. My stomach muscle clenched and I balled my toes up in my shoes. I had been tricked! Warren was already home!

"Didn't think you'd see me so soon, huh, Gianna, or should I call you Gigi Costner?" Warren spat, tightening his grip on my hair.

Tears were running down my face like a faucet. My body ached everywhere, but nothing compared to how much it hurt my heart to see him. The man I once loved was now getting ready to kill me. Warren's face was filled with hate, yet seeing him after all of these years made me still feel love for him. For the first time I truly regretted what I had done to him. I hadn't even called him after he was arrested. I didn't check for him while he did his bid, nor did I ever put one dollar in his commissary. I had essentially turned him in and left him for dead. Now, for the first time, I realized how serious that shit was in Warren's eyes. Especially since he had literally taken me out of the worst part of the hood and tried to give me a better life. I had shitted on him real bad. But in my eyes at the time, he had fucking shitted on me too.

"I'm . . . I'm . . . sorry," I gasped through tears.

Warren finally let my hair go with a shove. The force was so great the chair I was forced to sit in almost fell over. Warren was in my face again within seconds. "Did y'all hear this bitch? She said she was sorry!" Warren yelled out to the others in the room. They all started laughing, including Warren. I squinted until my eyes focused on his face. I saw pain etched on the worry line he'd acquired since going up North.

I could tell he was still weak for me. He didn't want to hurt me, but he was angry, so he had to prove a point, especially in front of his boys.

"Sorry?! You wasn't fucking sorry when you fucking snitched on me! You wasn't fucking sorry when you stole from me!" Warren screamed as he paced in front of me. "Not even one fucking visit while I was up North! Not even one dollar in my commissary! You are the worst kind of bitch! A bitch I trusted to be mine! I should've known a hood rat bitch like you wasn't about this life!" he barked. The veins in his neck pulsed fiercely and spit flew out of his mouth.

I was sobbing uncontrollably now. There was nothing I could say in response that would justify what I'd done. Warren's vituperative words were like open-handed slaps to my face. I think the words hurt worse than a slap would have. Within minutes Warren was back in my face. I was trembling with fear. He grabbed my face, his strong hand gripping both of my cheeks. He squeezed my face so hard I could feel my teeth making an impression on the inside of my cheeks. He forced me to look him in the eyes.

"You have twenty-four fucking hours to bring me those motherfuckin' diamonds or double what they were worth! If you try anything stupid . . . you and everything you love will die. If you think I'm fucking around . . . try me, Gianna," Warren gritted. He released my face and waved his hand. The next thing I knew someone was standing in front of me with an iPad shoved into my face. "Play with me if you want to, Gigi," Warren reiterated. The guy Warren had called over came quickly like a loyal servant. Warren pointed to something in the man's hand. The guy pressed a button on the iPad and forced me to watch the screen. My eyes widened at what I saw.

"Agggghh!!" I heard the screams coming from the computer device. That's when I saw the person screaming. It was my mother. She let out more blood-curdling screams as two masked men held guns to either side of her head. I lowered my head and sobbed uncontrollably. "Warren," I sobbed, barely able to speak. "Please . . . don't do this."

"Shut the fuck up and keep watching!" Warren said through clenched teeth. I let my eyes wander back to the screen. The fear in my mother's eyes made me wish I was dead for the danger I had put her in.

"Beg for your life! Beg, bitch!" the men who'd invaded my mother's home demanded. "Tell your daughter to play by the rules so you can live the rest of your life," one of the men commanded my mother.

"Gianna! Please!! Help me!! Give them whatever they want!" my mother cried out. I doubled over in response to her pain.

Suddenly the screen went black. "Please, Warren . . . you can't hurt her! Not after everything she has done for you! You can't hurt her! Just kill me, but don't hurt her!" I managed to scream through my burning throat.

"Oh, now you wanna worry about someone other than your fucking self? If you don't want to find her dead in that nice house you bought her with my fucking diamonds, you better find a way to either return my shit or repay me double of what they were worth," Warren demanded again with finality. Before I could even answer him, he flicked a card at me. I flinched thinking he was going to hit me again.

"That's how you get in touch with me. You better come up with a plan real fucking quick, bitch, because this time, I'm calling the fuckin' shots," Warren spat. His words sunk in on me and I felt hopeless. I didn't know what the fuck I was going to do, but I was going to have to come up with a plan. Maybe begging for mercy will work.

"Warren, I love you . . . please. Let's get back together. Please, baby. Spare me. I can make everything better. I can fix it all. I can get money from Sidney," I begged.

Warren let out a sinister, maniacal laugh. "Bitch, I don't care where you get the money from, but I better hear from you," he said.

My heart sunk as he hawked a wad of spit on me, then turned and walked away followed by his thugs. They were all laughing raucously as they left me in the strange warehouse-looking building all bruised and battered. At that moment, I wished like hell that Warren had just fucking killed me.

9

Scheming

On shaky legs, I got up from the chair I had been forced to sit in and walked in the direction Warren and his boys had gone. My body felt like I had been in a twelve-round boxing match with a heavyweight prizefighter. When I walked out into the fresh air, I bent over and threw up. It was a mixture of fear and overwhelming gratefulness that I was alive. The mere fact that I was still alive made me appreciate the air outside that much more. I knew that the only thing that probably kept Warren from offing me was the possibility of getting those diamonds back or at least the money for them. My insides churned, but not as much as my mind. I cried again when I saw that Warren had at least left my car there for me. I stumbled over to my car. Just as I was about to open the driver's side door, I noticed that my tires had been flattened. I'd forgotten they had shot my tires out when I first came to the stadium. He had left the car there as a joke . . . to taunt me, because he knew damn well I couldn't drive it like that. I looked around at the deserted, dark lot.

There was no one around for miles. I could hear the cars passing over top on Highway 264. There was no way anyone would even hear me screaming from down there.

"Fuck you, Warren! Fuck you!" I screamed, slamming my fists on the door. Lucky for me he had at least left the doors unlocked. I carefully climbed inside the vehicle and retrieved my cell phone. It was almost dead and there were at least twenty missed calls from my mother. There were also calls from Sidney. I didn't have time to listen to the voice messages. . . . I just wanted to use the little bit of battery life left to get the fuck out of there.

"Hello . . . um . . . can I get a cab to meet me in the parking lot of the Tides stadium? Yes! The parking lot . . . I have money to pay for it!" I screamed at the lady. She was acting like I was some damn crackhead trying to play games. It seemed like it took forever for the cab driver to find me, but he finally did. Of course he required that I pay upfront because he had picked me up in that seedy-ass area. "I need to go to the hospital," I told him.

"Are you all right?" he asked.

"Just mind your business and take me to the hospital!"

The cab took me straight to the Sentara Leigh Hospital. I exited the cab as fast as my battered body would allow. I looked up at the huge red sign that read, EMERGENCY ROOM. I staggered into the emergency room doors and all eyes were on me. I know I must've looked like shit. My hair had been pulled, my lips and eyes were swollen, bloodstains covered the front of my shirt. I looked around and located the nurse. I stumbled over to the triage station and leaned down on the small glass partition.

"Please help me . . . I've been attacked," I sobbed; then I slid down to the floor like I was hurt much worse than I had actually been beaten.

The nurse behind the glass jumped up just as I made myself lay flat on the floor. "Code yellow! Get me a gurney now! Code yellow!" I heard her yelling. It sounded like a million pairs of feet rushing toward me. I closed my eyes, finally feeling like I could let go and relax for a minute. I was quickly hoisted onto a gurney amid the hushed murmurs of the nurses and doctors who discussed my fate. I felt a bunch of hands probing me. They checked for a pulse, tested the rigidity of my abdomen, and shone a light into my eyes to see if my pupils were dilated. "She's been beaten pretty bad. Let's get a head CT and chest X-rays right away," I heard a doctor call out. I kept my eyes closed and let them cater to me. I knew there was much worse shit to come.

After all of the poking, prodding, X-rays, and CAT scans, I was finally placed into a hospital room. I was feeling better already from the pain medication I had been given. I kept rehearsing in my mind the story I was going to tell Sidney when he got there. The nurses had already notified him about my condition. I knew he would be completely falling apart until he got there. It seemed like an eternity before Sidney showed up at the hospital. I could hear him outside of my hospital room asking which room I was in. The heart monitor above my head began beeping as my heart rate sped up. It was time for me to deliver the lies I had conjured up in my head. I couldn't possibly tell Sidney the truth about what had happened. I was trying to think fast, but in my condition, that was no easy task.

"Oh, my God! Gigi! I'm so sorry! It's all my fault . . . I drove you from the house. This would've never happened if I hadn't argued with you," Sidney huffed as he rushed over to my bedside. Tears leaked out of the sides of my eyes and pooled in my ears. I don't know why the sight of Sidney and his words made me cry immediately. Maybe it was because I knew that it was really not his fault and that I was about to get him caught up in some shit.

"What happened, Gigi? Who did this to you?" he asked, grasping my hand tightly. I could see the strain of sympathy tugging at the sides of his eyes. It was time for me to tell my lies. I closed my eyes and inhaled deeply.

"I . . . I . . . stopped for gas and some guys . . ." I started, but I let the sobs flow freely. It was Academy Award–worthy acting, although I was still crying over the situation. "They . . . they just . . . attacked me," I sobbed.

"Shhhh. Don't worry about it. I know it's hard to talk about, but you will have to tell the police," Sidney said softly, stroking my hand. I snatched my hand away from him like a snake had bitten me. My slanted eyes went completely round. There was no way I could let the police get involved. They would be snooping and asking too many fucking questions! No way!

"No!" I raised my voice. "I don't want the police involved. The guys took my identification and told me if I get the police involved, they would kill me and you," I fabricated on the spot.

Sidney looked at me like I was crazy. He stood up, his back stiff and erect. I always knew when he was uncomfortable with a situation. His face was serious, angry even.

"Gigi, there is no fucking way I'm going to allow anyone to get away with what they did to you! If you don't want the cops involved, then I will hire someone to look for these punks, but it can't go unspoken just like that! They fucking put their hands on you and I am your husband . . . I'm not going to just let them get away with this!" Sidney said through clenched teeth.

I swallowed hard and closed my eyes. I knew he wasn't going to let this go. I had to think quickly. "Okay . . . if you want to hire someone to look for them. But, you know I don't trust the police. I don't want them involved," I said. Sidney seemed to calm down, but the look he gave me said he was suspicious of my story already.

I was released from the hospital the next morning. The doctors had notified the police anyway since they claimed they were mandated reporters as medical caregivers. When the cops showed up, I told them I couldn't remember anything . . . that I just woke up on the ground after some guys beat me up and took my car at the gas station. They seemed suspicious, but they didn't press. Of course, they had found my vehicle with nothing missing from it, so they wanted to know why it was in the stadium parking lot. I had to literally scream at them that I didn't know because the guys had stolen it. They didn't have any store surveillance showing a carjacking they had said. I screamed at them so bad they went hightailing away from me. They had even informed

Sidney that my tires had been shot out. Sidney seemed suspicious of me as well, so he enlisted a guy named Ricco who worked for him to sit outside of the house and "keep an eye on me." That frustrated me, but I understood where Sidney was coming from. He stayed with me a few hours, then told me he had things to do at the business.

Damn, he couldn't leave soon enough. I knew I had to get in touch with Warren or else. As soon as Sidney went to take care of business, I dialed the number Warren had told me to call. I had no choice . . . there was only about six more hours until my twenty-four hours were up. I was fucking trembling as I waited for Warren to pick up the line. I paced the floor of my bedroom and kept peeking out of the windows like a paranoid crazy person. Finally, he picked up.

"G-money . . . I knew you'd be obedient. You ain't that fucking stupid now, are you," Warren said when he answered the phone. He got right to the point. "So, you scheming-ass bitch . . . what's the plan to get me my money or those diamonds back?" I exhaled.

"I don't have anything, Warren. I don't have the diamonds and I don't have any money. I don't have access to my husband's accounts like that. He gives me an allowance, but I know he keeps at least five hundred thousand in the safe at the dealership," I whispered tentatively, my voice quivering.

Warren started laughing like I had said something real funny. I crinkled my eyebrows in response. He stopped laughing abruptly and started talking in a very serious tone. "Yo . . . you really don't know what you did, huh? You are fucking clueless that you stole twenty rare, precious diamonds belonging to Sensi Akiwaba . . . a fucking warlord from Sierra Leone! You don't know this muthafucka has had people's hands and arms cut the fuck off for stealing his diamonds! How you think I'm out here??? That nigga paid the best lawyers in town to get me out just so I could find you, Gigi! You are the most wanted bitch in America right now! And guess what? If I don't return those fucking diamonds or at least four million dollars, you are fucking dead!" Warren barked.

I listened intently, letting his words settle into my brain. It all hit me at once. I felt like someone had hit me in the head with a lead fucking pipe. Warren had just dropped a big bomb on me. I had stolen from the wrong muthafuckas for sure. I had no idea that Warren had been doing business with the Africans. I had heard back when I lived in DC that the Africans had been taking over DC at the time with pure heroin and meth, but I never put two and two together about the diamonds. I never knew I was in deep shit like that. I could really just kill my mother for staying in contact with Warren. It was all because of her that I was in this situation now! Who was I fooling? Those Africans probably would have found me with or without Warren's help. I was walking around a wanted woman and I didn't even know it!

"So what am I supposed to do, Warren? I don't know if Sidney has that kind of money just lying around," I said through tears. I knew Sidney was pretty wealthy, but I was sure he probably had his shit invested or in overseas accounts. I was so much younger than Sidney, having him killed for insurance money wasn't an option. That would be a sure way to get myself investigated. Plus, I figured I might be beneficiary on one of his policies, but most of his shit was probably going to go to his kids. My mind was racing at a mile a minute.

"Don't ask me what the fuck you should do. You didn't ask me what to do when you stole the shit from my crib!" Warren replied with a lot of base in his voice. "You better fucking come up with something and fast. I guess you will have to do something drastic to get the money . . . I don't care if you rob a fucking bank . . . you better start thinking," Warren said. His words caused a chill to take over my body.

"I'll come up with something. But after you get your money I want you to leave us alone," I cried.

Warren let out a crazy laugh again. "I'll leave you alone when I'm ready, bitch. Now you're going to help me get this money from your man or else," he said.

I came up with an idea that quickly. I knew there were very few things that were more important to Sidney than his own life. "I have an idea, but it will have to be well thought out. You will have to do it quick and swift," I told Warren.

"I'm listening," he said. I started talking and there was silence on the other end of the phone. I began to lay out a plan with Warren that would save my own ass. Just like that, I was scheming right along with Warren.

10

Betrayal

I paced inside the house waiting for Warren's call. I had told him all he needed to know to go through with the plan, but he was insisting that I go with him. When he said that, my mind started to race because Sidney had one of his boys outside the house. I asked Ricco to run and pick me up some takeout; he was hesitant, and asked me not to tell Sidney, but he went. As soon as his ass pulled out of our circular driveway I was right behind him.

Warren picked me up around the corner from my estate. It was a crazy feeling knowing that Warren knew where I rested my head every night. He knew everything. I was shaking like a leaf in a windstorm when I got into the car with him. I didn't know if he was going to beat me up again or something even worse this time. I slid into the seat and didn't dare look over at Warren. We were alone in the car, but I'm sure he wasn't alone altogether. I was sure he had his dudes hiding out somewhere ready to pounce.

"Dayum, G-money, I ain't mean to bruise that pretty face like that," Warren said, his voice sly and sarcastic.

The nerve of this bastard! I stared straight ahead without a word. We didn't need to be friendly. I was just going to try to get this shit resolved. Warren reached over and ran his hand gently over my cheek. I jumped and my heart started thumping fiercely against my chest bone. I was so scared and paranoid, not to mention my body still throbbed from what Warren and Ace had done to me.

"Please, Warren," I murmured, moving my head so that my face was far from his touch. I didn't want any physical contact with him.

"Shhh, I'm not going to hurt you anymore," Warren said softly. It was like he was crazy. One minute he was trying to damn near kill me, now he wanted to be all nice? I didn't trust his ass one bit. Back when we were together I would've never believed that he would ever put his hands on me the way he did the other day.

"You gotta feel where I'm coming from. I was left behind the walls, dead and stinking, and you stole from me . . . on the real, I wanted to murk you as soon as I saw you, but I couldn't," he continued.

As hard as I tried to fight off the feeling, I started to feel fuzzy inside when he spoke. Although he had hurt me, something inside of me still felt for Warren. No matter what, I guess he would always occupy a part of my heart as my first real love. I wanted to believe that he was angry when he'd put his hands on me. That he would've never really wanted to hurt me like that. It didn't matter anyway, he had already done it. I was wearing the scars to show it too.

"I'm sorry, Warren. I didn't mean it, but I was scared and left with no one and nothing when the feds got us. They told me that you were blaming me for everything . . . I saw you on video," I was finally able to explain. I was still too scared to look at him.

Warren reached over and grabbed me. "Aggh, please!" I screamed. I just knew another beating was coming.

"G-money . . . G-money . . . c'mon, I'm not going to hurt you. I would've never blamed you for anything. You don't know about the feds and their video tricks? That was all game, baby girl," Warren said, pulling my head toward his. I stopped resisting for just a second. Warren pulled my face into his. I was shocked. He kissed me so deeply that I could barely breathe. I couldn't even fight him off if I wanted to and I didn't even try. Although I was deathly afraid, it felt so good to feel Warren's tongue in my mouth again. Tears drained out of the sides of my bruised eyes. I was conflicted as hell. On the one hand, I hated him because everything that was wrong in my life was because of him. But I knew then that I still loved that man no matter what. It was all for nothing, though. We were about to do some shit that would never allow us to be together again.

Finally, I pulled away from him. "Damn, G-money . . . we could've been so good together," Warren lamented with finality. He pulled his car away from the curb and we both rode to do the deed in eerie silence.

I immediately noticed that there was a black SUV following us. It wasn't a surprise. I surmised that it was the same SUV that had been parked at the Tides stadium the night I was set up and assaulted. I can't say seeing that vehicle didn't make my insides curl in on themselves.

"So where we going?" Warren asked. I'd been so lost in thought he startled me. I blinked a few times and was back on course with what we were doing.

"She's usually at school at this time. Tidewater Community College," I said, my voice quivering. "She has a red Honda Z sports car. Her plates say daddy's little girl." I knew this was the ultimate betrayal, but what choice did I have?

"Her daddy is rich and she goes to community college?" Warren asked skeptically. He sounded as if he was trying to smooth the tension between us in the car. I just shrugged. The less conversation we had the better for me.

"It's all just like I said. The time, the place, and the same pattern every day," I whispered. I wasn't trying to be Warren's friend and chitchat about the girl I was about to turn into a victim. After all, she was my stepdaughter.

"A'ight. And you sure daddy ain't gon' call five-o to get his baby back? I'm not about to play no bullshit . . . I will murk you, her, and him and move the fuck on," Warren said. That was the Warren I expected to hear. It was like his mood had gone from day to night. I guess he was back to hating my guts.

"I'm sure," I said, my voice unsteady. I wasn't sure of shit. Sidney was a businessman, not a gangster, so there was a high probability he might call the cops or even the fucking FBI. I was saying a silent prayer that Sidney didn't try any funny business once he received the ransom demand. I was also praying that God spared my ass for this foul shit I was doing.

I watched the whole shit unfold after I pointed Arianna out to Warren. I had to admit, Warren's boys were like pros. It all happened so fast. I watched from a distance as one of Ace's boys slyly put a gun to Arianna's back, whispered in her ear not to scream, made her get into her own car and he got in the passenger seat. The last thing I said to Warren was, "Remember, she's just a kid. Her father will pay the ransom, so don't hurt her." He looked at me with fire flashing in his evil eyes. "I guess that's your job now. Convince daddy to play by the rules and the girl goes home. Play games and everybody goes to hell together," Warren replied before he put me out of his car.

Sidney's first call came forty-five minutes after I did the deed with Warren. I had been dropped back to my car before the call came in. I picked up my cell phone with shaky hands. I closed my eyes and asked God to forgive me for everything I was doing.

"Hello? Hey, baby," I said with a phony voice. I could hear the nerves in my own words, but I don't think Sidney did. I had to pull the phone away from my ear because Sidney was yelling so loud. A cold feeling came over me like I had been pushed into an icy river. My bottom lip trembled. I knew I was going to hell for this.

"Gigi! Gigi!" he was screaming. I closed my eyes. I didn't realize I had been holding my breath. I felt fucking awful inside.

"Gigi . . . I need you to go into my safe at home!" Sidney sounded frantic and like he was crying. This shit was real, but I still pinched myself to make sure I wasn't having a nightmare.

"Sidney . . . why are you yelling? What is going on?" I asked, acting stupid.

"Gigi!" Sidney cried out again. "Listen to me!!"

"What?! Tell me what is going on! Stop calling my name and tell me what's going on!" I yelled back. I needed to let my fear and frustration out, so this was the perfect cover.

"Somebody has Arianna! Somebody snatched her! They said if I don't give them four million dollars, she dies! They said if I go to the police, they will send me her body in a suitcase," Sidney sobbed. He was coming completely undone. I felt my stomach drop. I closed my eyes and for just that minute, although I hated his kids, I felt kind of bad that this was all my doing. All to save my own ass from Warren.

"Oh, my God, Sidney! I think we should go to the police!" I yelped real phony-like. I only said that because I knew that would be the logical thing to say if I weren't down with the kidnapping. Any normal stepmother would say call the cops.

"No! Absolutely not! I will give them every dime I have to save my daughter's life!" Sidney screamed at me. That kind of made me feel bad. He really was a good person.

"Okay. Okay. Whatever you think is best," I quickly agreed, relieved that he wasn't going to mess up the plan by involving the police. I knew he was smarter than that.

"Calm down and tell me the safe combination," I told him. Sidney had never trusted me enough before now to give me the combination to the safe that held his money. I was thinking good for his ass for not trusting me, but I kept my smart remarks to myself. Who knew this would be the circumstances it took to get into that damn big money safe. I had often wondered just how much money Sidney kept inside of the safe. I guess I was about to find out. Sidney rattled off the numbers and I punched them in on the safe's digital lock pad. It didn't work the first time.

"Are you sure you gave me the right numbers?" I asked. I heard Sidney breathe hard into the phone. "Honey, calm down and think first," I told him. He rattled off another number combination. I punched those in and the little red light finally turned green on the safe. I turned the heavy metal knob and heard the lock give with a click. It was finally open. I pulled back the door to reveal the contents. My eyes lit up like a kid at Christmas when I pulled back that door and saw all of the cash Sidney had inside. I felt flush being exposed to that money. Money was the root of all evil, and trust me, all kinds of evil thoughts were running through my head at that moment.

"This muthafucka is truly fucking rich," I mouthed silently. I grabbed a few of the stacks of cash out of the safe, held them up to my nose, and inhaled deeply. The smell of the money was intoxicating to say the least. It was the smell of freedom. I was in a stupor. I felt nostalgic holding that money. It was like old times again when I had my own money. I forgot I was even on the phone with Sidney, that's how lost I was in the idea of that money in my hands.

"Gigi . . . there should be about five hundred thousand in those stacks there," Sidney said, interrupting my daze. I blinked at the sound of his voice. The amount of money in my hand didn't help keep my nerves at bay either.

"You sure? There seems to be less," I lied as I rushed around the closet secreting a few stacks of cash inside three of my handbags. It was foul, I know, but so was all the other shit I've had to do over the years to survive. I figured that the cash, along with the few remaining diamonds, should secure my escape after all of this shit with Warren blew over. I wasn't stupid enough to think that after this shit I could just continue to live my life as Mrs. Sidney Costner, happy wife. Plus, my mother was a wreck these days. Especially after she found out that I had also been assaulted. She was swearing to God that someone was going to kill us. I had told her to go stay with her best friend from church way out in the country, so I wasn't worried about her at that minute, but I knew I would have to make a plan for her as well.

Things had gone from real good to real bad within a matter of days. I started realizing that Warren had always been right at the helm of everything that had ever gone bad in my life. When I walked out of college, it was because of Warren. The first time I got pregnant and had an abortion, it was by Warren. The first time I stayed out overnight without calling my mother, it was with Warren. And the biggest failure was getting arrested by the fucking feds because of some shit Warren had told me to do. Now, I was perpetrating the worst form of betrayal you could ever think of and why . . . because of Warren. Warren was a fucking bad omen in my life. Even now that there was a very strong possibility he was going to get his money for the diamonds back and then some, I still had a feeling that Warren was going to try some funny business even after he got his fucking money to pay the Africans. He seemed to have to cover for his actions, so him killing me and my mother wasn't that far from my thoughts.

"Gigi, look again. I can't remember taking anything out of there. I always kept the same amount in there just in case I ever need it for the business and can't get to the bank," Sidney said. I let out a long, exasperated breath.

"I don't have time to count all of this money. I'm just saying it doesn't seem like the amount you said," I replied, annoyed.

"Okay, whatever it is . . . just put it in a bag and meet me at the dealership. Tell Ricco to bring you. They want the money by midnight or else they'll do something bad to Arianna. I have to call my accountant and try to get my hands on some more money or else my baby girl will be dead by morning," Sidney said nervously.

"Okay, I'll be right there," I said. I grabbed one of his big travel duffel bags and stacked the money inside. There was something overwhelmingly powerful about picking up a duffel bag filled with stacks of cash. So much so that I felt dizzy at first. God knows I wanted to take the fucking money, go get my mother, and get the fuck out of dodge. I could just leave and let Sidney and Warren hash out their problems. If Warren murdered Arianna as a result, oh well, I never liked her anyway. I could take the money and do better than I did with the proceeds of the diamonds. Yeah, that's what I'd do . . . take that fucking money and disappear, but this time to some place in another country. Fuck it!

All of that was on my mind and I was really close to going through with it, but I thought better of it. Being the most wanted woman in America wasn't on my list of life accomplishments. I guess I also had a little more heart than to just completely fuck Sidney over after all he'd done for me. Besides, I didn't want to be on the run the rest of my life. Those years I spent watching my back all of the time after I ran from DC was stressful enough. Funny thing was, as soon as I eased up with watching my back, Warren found me. Life was crazy like that, I guess.

11

Diamonds Are Forever

I walked downstairs with the bag of money clutched tightly in my hand. This was supposed to be a foolproof plan. We'd get as much money from Sidney as possible to get the Africans off our backs; then Warren would leave me the fuck alone forever. I could only pray it would go that smoothly.

"Ricco, I need a ride to the lot," I told Sidney's bodyguard who'd been outside of my house. He eyed me up and down, his eyes finally landing on the duffel bag. I shot him a look that said, "Don't even fucking ask." We rode in silence all the way there. I knew we had a tail and I think Ricco knew too.

When Ricco and I arrived at the dealership, I turned to him and told him, "Sidney said you can leave without coming inside." Ricco had that same suspicious look on his face. I guess that's what made him a good bodyguard, but I wasn't up for that shit today. Whether it was guilt written all over me or not, I didn't feel like having his beady-ass disapproving eye on me.

"Mrs. Costner, are you sure everything is all right?" Ricco

asked. I was taken aback by his question. Couldn't believe he had the balls to come out with it.

"Everything is fine. I told you this already," I snapped at him. "Oh, and I won't tell Sidney anything about you leaving me to go get food earlier if you don't," I followed up. I knew that would chill him and make him back off. Ricco knew he wasn't supposed to leave me under any circumstances. I was sure he didn't want Sidney to know that shit. Ricco nodded. Of course, he called Sidney to verify that he was no longer needed before he pulled away from the dealership. Yes, he was that loyal.

I rushed inside where I found Sidney in the entire place alone. He was in his office pacing like a mad man. He wore the pain and stress on his face like a mask. I tried my best to look just as stressed so he would think I was feeling his pain. He turned around and stopped for a minute when I walked in. His face softened just a bit. I guess my presence made him feel somewhat better. It made me feel worse. I was wrestling between self-satisfaction and guilt. I had done the most fucked-up thing to a man who had been nothing but good to me from day one. On the other hand, it was a means to an end.

"Gigi . . . I can't believe someone would do this to me. To my family. My fucking kid? I help everyone in the community. . . . I am nothing but good to these thugs that come in here flaunting their drug money. . . . I can't believe this is happening to me," he said sadly, grabbing me in a tight embrace.

I tried not to feel bad, but I was actually dying inside. I held on to Sidney just as tightly as he held me. I prayed silently that this shit would be over very soon. Arianna would be returned to Sidney, Warren would have his money, and I could sneak away in the thick of the night with the remaining diamonds and some of Sidney's cash. That's how I envisioned everything going.

"I'm so sorry, Sidney. I'm so sorry," I said softly. I meant that in more than one way. "So what did they say?" I asked as I eyed all of the cash Sidney had stacked on his desk.

Sidney pulled away from me. He rushed over to the desk and picked something up. "Look at this," Sidney instructed as he turned his laptop around so I could see the screen. More fucking videos! I stared at the screen, unable to look away, but wishing I could.

"Daddy!!!! Daddy!!! Please come get me!! Help me, Daddy!" Arianna screamed at the top of her lungs. Her hands and feet were bound with silver duct tape and there was a black bag over her head. Her screams were slightly muffled by the bag, but her words seemed to be amplified and crystal clear. There were guns pointed at either side of her head. Her captors didn't say anything; I guess the scene spoke volumes. Just as abruptly as it had started, it had ended. The screen went black, but I kept staring at it. Although it was black now, the image of Arianna was still showing clearly in my eyes. I didn't even realize that I had placed my hand over my mouth. I guess planning something like that and actually seeing it live and in living color was totally different. I can't front, that video had taken my breath away. Only a really coldhearted person wouldn't have been chilled by that shit. I knew I was a lot of things, but a person devoid of feelings I was not. Sidney's kids had treated me like shit the handful of times I'd seen them, especially Arianna, but seeing her all bound up, screaming for her life, and scared to death like that sent chills down my spine. Knowing that it was all my doing made me want to fucking faint. What if Warren kills her anyway? What if he takes the money, then kills her, me, and Sidney just to send a message? What if he's already killed my mother? My mind raced crazy. Maybe this wasn't the most well-thought-out fucking plan after all. I had left Warren in the prime position to be the one calling the shots.

"So what do we do now?" I asked. Shit, now I had taken Sidney's place at pacing the floor. I knew Warren and Ace couldn't give a fuck about Sidney or his daughter. They wanted that money and that was it.

"I'm waiting for them to call back," Sidney said, flopping down on the leather couch in his office. He held his head in his hands. "I don't have all of the money. All I could come up with on such short notice was one point five million," Sidney said, worry lacing his words. That wasn't good fucking news. The hairs on my arms stood straight up.

"Do you think you can buy some time?" I asked, trying to stay calm. "Do you have the rest someplace else that you can get to if you ask for more time?" I continued, my voice rising a few octaves. I had assured Warren that Sidney would get the money with ease, hand it over, and it would all be over. Now shit seemed like it wasn't going to go so easily.

Sidney looked at me through squinted eyes. The look on his face kind of scared me. "This is all so strange, Gigi. No one knows where my kids live. None of my partners or the guys I do business with have ever seen my kids. I don't have enemies. I don't advertise my wealth to attract anyone. So how would anyone know I could even try to get that much money? Someone had to follow me to see the kids, but Arianna wasn't home, so even if they did . . . how would someone know her movements? I don't ever put them on display for the world to see. Something about this isn't right," Sidney speculated.

I swallowed hard before I even tried to speak. He was right. It was something I didn't think about. Sidney was a very private guy aside from his business dealings.

"Now is not the time to come up with some conspiracy theory, Sidney. Arianna is a very flashy girl. You know she loves to flaunt her car and her expensive clothes, bags, and shoes. This might be some thug she met trying to shake you down for money. Look, maybe we should just call the cops," I said, walking toward the telephone on his desk. If he wanted to speculate, I could play that game too. I had to be convincing.

Sidney jumped up and was on me faster than a flash. I don't think I'd ever seen his old ass move that fast. He grabbed me by my neck. My eyes popped open as I gagged. Sidney squeezed tightly. He was like a possessed demon. I had never seen him like that at all.

"I said you will not call the cops! I want to get my daughter back in one piece. Now don't fucking try to pick up that phone again," Sidney said through clenched teeth. I swore I could see pure fire flashing in Sidney's eyes. When he let go of my neck I had no choice but to cough uncontrollably to try and catch my breath.

Just as I got my lungs to fill back up with air, Sidney's phone rang. We both almost jumped out of our skin. Sidney answered it. I was all ears. I knew it had to be Warren. I also knew Sidney didn't have all of the money, so I was wondering what Warren would do when Sidney told him.

"Arianna! Baby!" I heard Sidney cry out. I closed my eyes and listened to the girl's cries filter through the phone. My stomach churned. I was biting my nails down to the quick at that point.

"I'm trying my best, baby! I'm going to get you out of there! I don't care what I have to do. I'm not going to let them hurt you," Sidney was saying. Suddenly his tone of voice changed. Warren and his goons must've taken the phone away from Arianna because I could tell right away Sidney was no longer talking to her. He turned his back to me and was silent for a few minutes as he listened to whatever they were saying. Just when I couldn't take the suspense any longer, he said, "Just tell me where you want to meet! I have all of the money! Just don't hurt her!" Sidney pleaded. He had just fucking lied to dangerous-ass Warren and Ace. My jaw went slack and I looked at Sidney like he was crazy. Sidney was about to play with niggas who were not to be fucked with. I couldn't even warn him, but damn if I didn't want to scream at his ass. I was shaking my head. Sidney was bugging the fuck out for sure. He just didn't know what the fuck he was doing.

"Sidney?! How can you lie to them?! What the hell are you going to do showing up to meet them without the whole four million dollars!" I gasped after he hung up the phone. I was gnawing on my bottom lip so hard I eventually tasted my own blood.

"Don't worry about that. I know what I'm doing and I'm

not going to let anything happen to my daughter. I would die first before I let these hood motherfuckers hurt my kid," Sidney said with conviction. He seemed much calmer, yet much more ruthless than he had been. Something about his sudden change in behavior made me feel uneasy inside. I couldn't place it, but it seemed to me like Sidney knew more than he was letting on. I shook my head quickly, shaking off my paranoia. I ignored that nagging feeling inside of me. My mother had always said, trust your first instinct, it will never steer you wrong. Well, I ignored mine . . . which would end up being my worst mistake.

12

Turning the Tables

"Let's go, Gigi!" Sidney huffed as he stuffed the stacks of money he had taken from the dealership into the bag of money I had brought from the house. I just followed his lead at that point. If he thought he could take less than a million dollars and fool his daughter's kidnappers, then who was I to argue. I couldn't keep convincing him to get more money because I was afraid he would get too suspicious of me. "You ready?" he asked me. My eyebrows went high into arches.

"You want me to go with you?" I asked, my voice going higher.

"Yes, I'm not going to take a chance with you being here or home alone and something happening to you too," Sidney replied. Something about his voice was eerie ... fake even, but what choice did I have now given the circumstances. I let out a long sigh. This also wasn't part of what I had envisioned for what was supposed to be a very simple ransom demand. I guess when it came to crime and money nothing was fucking simple.

I followed Sidney to the first level of the dealership. He didn't go toward the front door. "We are leaving through the repair shop. Can't take a chance with anyone following us," Sidney told me. We were leaving through the back, which faced nothing but highway and trees. Sidney was a little more street smart than I'd pegged him to be.

My jaw fell open when we walked outside. There were two darkly tinted cars filled with niggas sitting outside. The driver of each car stepped out to speak with Sidney. They surely looked like hardened thugs.

"We got everything we need," one very dark-skinned dude told Sidney. The other guy who looked like he ate, slept, and shit weights nodded at Sidney. I crinkled my eyebrows and looked at Sidney.

"What are you doing, Sidney?" My stomach churned so hard I felt like my sphincter muscle would give out on the spot.

"I'm going to get my fucking daughter back. Those pieces of shit said not to call the police, but I have people just like they do. I do good for these guys. They didn't even fucking blink when I told them I needed them," Sidney retorted.

He had transformed into someone I didn't even recognize. He was like a mafia goon all of a sudden. Certainly not the refined gentleman I had met and married.

"Let's go!" he said to me, pushing me toward his car. My nerves were completely exposed. My hands were no good. They shook so badly I could barely open the car door to get in. Things were not going to be cut and dry, that much I could see. I wanted to warn Warren, but Sidney was watching me like a hawk. There was no way I could've pulled out my cell phone at that point. I closed my eyes, prayed for mercy, and prepared for the worst.

The drive to the meeting spot seemed like it took an eternity. I couldn't keep my legs from rocking in and out. When we arrived, I looked around and took in the nightmarish scene. It was another dark, desolate place that I didn't recognize, but it was near the water. From the scent in the air and the heavy breeze I was guessing we were somewhere close to the beach. When Sidney and I drove down the small, winding road, I didn't see the cars with his people in them behind us.

"What is the plan, Sidney?" I asked tentatively. He was being pin-drop quiet.

"To get Arianna back," Sidney replied dryly. I looked out of the window and noticed the same SUV from the night of my assault sitting in the distance. I knew it was Warren and Ace. I also knew they wouldn't be alone. They'd have their people hiding somewhere just like Sidney did. My heartbeat quickened and I suddenly felt like my bladder would release involuntarily.

"C'mon," Sidney instructed as he shut the car off. I looked at him like he was crazy. My heart jerked in my chest. Is he fucking crazy?!

"Me? Why do I need to get out? You said you didn't want to put me in harm's way. Just give them the money, get Arianna, and get back in the car," I exclaimed, looking at him like he was crazy. Things were spiraling downward fast. I didn't know how I would react being face-to-face with Warren and Sidney. There was no way I was getting out of the fucking car!

"They said they want everybody in the car to get out. I guess they don't want to take a chance on you calling the cops or doing anything funny," Sidney explained. Still, something about his behavior was off; he didn't seem nervous enough to be a father going to pay ransom for his child. He kept saying everything was going to be all right. I guess at that time it all sounded logical enough. It also sounded like something Warren would've demanded, since I knew Warren to trust no one.

Sidney reached into the back seat and grabbed the bag of money. I knew there was a little less than one million in the bag . . . not enough. I shook my head side to side. Sidney and I stepped out of his car. My legs felt like butter against the sun. I saw the doors of the SUV swing open. Ace and another dude stepped out, but I didn't see Warren or Arianna. I looked over at Sidney. He had a mean mug on his face. He was definitely a man I didn't recognize at that point. He never looked at me, nor did he say a word to me. In fact, it was like I was no longer there. He started walking toward Ace with the bag and I moved slowly behind him. I felt like throwing up. The anticipation of what was to come was killing me inside.

"Where's my daughter?!" Sidney called out. Ace started laughing.

"Where's the money?!" Ace called back.

Sidney lifted the bag up as if to say "right here."

Ace nodded.

Sidney kept walking toward the SUV. The other dude went around the back of the vehicle. I squeezed my eyes shut when I saw them bring Arianna from the back of the vehicle. She was dressed nicely. There was no bag over her head nor were her hands bound.

"Arianna baby! Are you all right?! Did they hurt you?!" Sidney called out.

"Daddy!!" Arianna responded. Sidney and Arianna were smiling as they ran into each other to embrace.

"Police!! Nobody move!!" I heard loud screams. Next, it was like a herd of wild elephants moving toward me. I whirled around on the balls of my feet and my eyes widened as far as they could go. Here I was again. I was surrounded by gun-toting law enforcement in black raid jackets.

"Gianna Costner, you are under arrest for the attempted kidnapping and attempted murder of Arianna Costner!" I heard one of the police call out.

My body felt hot all over. I felt like I could just faint.

"What is going on?! I didn't kidnap anyone! You want him!" I screeched, turning toward Warren.

Warren had a smirk on his face. His arms were folded over his chest in a smug display of satisfaction.

"Sidney! Tell them! Tell them, honey! Tell them what happened!" I screamed, turning toward my husband. Sidney looked at me through squinted eyes, his nostrils flared feverishly.

"What's going on is the tables have turned on you. I can't believe how low you would stoop. You really believed that you could have my daughter kidnapped for ransom money to repay your debt? I wish I could fucking blow your head off right here . . . right now!" Sidney said angrily.

At that point, I saw movement from my peripheral vision. I looked over. Arianna moved closer to her father. She was scowling at me, but something in her eyes seemed to say, "Ha-ha, bitch." Even she had been a part of the setup.

"Good work, Warren," one of the police said to Warren, clapping him on the shoulder like a proud father would his son. My jaw almost dropped. I looked from Warren over to Sidney, then to the police. I didn't know how to react. I felt rage boiling up inside me as two officers began grabbing me to handcuff me.

"What the fuck is this?!" I snapped angrily. It was all I could do to keep myself from dying on the spot. "Why are you all doing this to me?! Warren is a fucking criminal! Sidney! He made me do it! He threatened to kill you and my mother! You have to believe me! I wasn't going to let anything happen to Arianna!" I screamed as I began flailing my arms to prevent them from putting me in handcuffs. "I didn't do anything! It's not me! He is the kidnapper!" I screamed as I pointed at Warren accusingly. It was like he was happy to see me like this. My arms were grabbed roughly and forced behind my back. "Ouch!" I cried out. Tears started streaming down my face. I was confused and I felt like my chest would explode. The cops started pushing me toward a squad car. "Warren! Tell them the truth!!"

Warren followed behind me. The officers turned me around to face him. I stared at his evil face as he spoke.

"See, G-money . . . two can play that snitching game,

baby girl. You think I got out early for good behavior? They don't let niggas like me back in the world unless we got something to offer them. At first, it was all about taking down your man for his shady dealings. . . . I thought that would hurt him and then in turn it would hurt you. But I realized real fast that you was the same ol' G-money . . . you ain't give a shit about that man. You don't love him . . . never did . . . never will.

"I tested the waters on you and it worked. You got tripped up in there and I couldn't resist the fucking revenge. They got it all on tape, ma. When we told Sidney what you did to his kid and about this plan to take your ass down, he was down for it. He knew about what you did all along. He just didn't know how low you'd stoop to save yourself . . . how selfish you really are. I guess I always knew firsthand . . . them four years in the joint told it all," Warren said, his words hitting me like hard slaps to the face.

It was all a setup, starting with Ace showing up at the dealership that day. Things started ringing bells in my head, but it was too late now. With them having me on tape pointing out Arianna the day of the kidnapping, there was probably nothing a defense attorney could do for me. I was speechless. Then I heard more screams.

"I can't believe you, Gigi! I can't believe I ever loved you! I feel like shooting you right here!" Sidney shouted, moving toward me. The police converged on him to keep him away from me. I could see the hurt in his eyes. He really had loved me when no one else did. I felt like shit inside for what I'd done. He was right . . . all to save myself. I truly was wishing one of them would just go ahead and shoot me already.

The cops were getting a kick out of the fucking soap opera taking place, too, because they just kept me there dying slowly.

"Please . . . Please! I didn't know it would go this far! You have to believe me! You have to understand!" I pleaded. I could see my pleas didn't do a thing to sway any of them. Sidney's face turned dark. Then he let out a high-pitched, evil, maniacal laugh that sent cold chills straight down my spine. He stepped closer to me. So close I could smell his breath.

"I hope you like it in hell," Sidney whispered in my face. Next I felt my head being forced down as I was roughly placed into the waiting squad car. My life was over and I'd no longer be calling the shots. Once again, Warren was a fucking bad omen in my life.

On Da Run

Nikki Turner

1

Four of a Kind

Beauty Boutique smelled like hairspray, oil sheen, relaxers, and pressed hair. The shop was supposed to close at 9:00 p.m. on Friday nights. However, the staff—a half-dozen dedicated beauticians, barbers, massage therapist, and stylists, including the owner—didn't normally make it out of the building until after eleven, even if they were lucky. Like most urban salons doing relaxers, coloring, and extensions, the later part of the week was when they made the majority of their paper.

And there was no denying Peaches Brown, the sole proprietor, was definitely about her money. Being a highly sought-after makeup artist and esthetician didn't begin to describe Peaches's skills with makeup and hair. Her techniques were so good, clients swore that having Peaches do your makeup was like using special effects, and she could outdo any transformation you've seen on a TV show. But as good as Peaches was with her makeup and hair brushes, she also used her talented hands to hold her own at poker tables.

Her father, Mickey, had taught her the game of skill and nerve when she was just seven years old. He used to tell her that a good poker player can read the cards and calculate the correct percentage bet in less time than it took a square to glance at a pretty girl. "But the great ones," he made a point to let Peaches know, "read the opponent first." He would tell her, "The card isn't anywhere near as important to you if you've already read the person playing 'em." And over the years she learned to do this well.

By the time Peaches turned twelve, she was deeply in love with the game of poker. By her fifteenth birthday, she could pull up a seat next to the best underground players in the city . . . reason being she was simply one of the best herself.

A friend of her father's had called only minutes ago to tell her about an exclusive gathering that was by invite only. The only way she could attend was if she canceled all of her late-evening appointments. She prided herself in valuing her customers' time and felt bad that she had to leave early. As she put the finishing touches on her client currently in her chair, she kept thinking how she was going to explain to her clients that someone else would be serving them. She turned her customer Malika around and handed her a mirror.

"How do you like it? I filled your eyebrows in some. Stop trying to arch them in yourself, okay, because it is a mess for me to try to clean up."

Malika looked over the beautiful makeup job in the mirror. "I like this, Ms. Peaches. You have me looking like a supermodel. I'm going to have all eyes on me tonight."

"And that you will."

She rose up from the chair, admiring herself in the big

wall mirror. "Come on, Ms. Peaches." Malika whipped her phone out and snapped a picture of herself. She pursed her lips. "I have to Instagram this for sure so the people can know who the lady with the baddest makeup brush in the land is."

"That's so sweet of you," Peaches said as she leaned in for the snapshot.

"You know I'm gonna tag you on the post," she said, digging in her Tory Burch purse to pay Peaches.

"Thank you," she said as she took the cash from Malika. "Just remember what I said, stop with the at-home eyebrow shaving, please," Peaches said, hoping Malika would do as she requested.

"I hear you, Ms. Peaches." She smiled. "And make sure you like our flick on Instagram," she said as she exited the shop.

Peaches looked at her iPhone and read the time. She needed to get out of there if she was going to be on time.

"Oh, my sweet Janika, I need a favor," Peaches said, pulling the voluptuous woman away from her client that she was about to put under the dryer. Janika had worked for Peaches since the shop opened two years ago. She didn't have a quarter of the clients Peaches had, but she was at that shop from sunup to sundown, helping out and soaking up all the knowledge she could from the other stylist in the shop.

"What's up, Peaches? I know that voice. What exactly do you need me to do?"

"I have to go somewhere and I need you to take care of two of my clients coming in. You know I'ma hook you up tomorrow. Okay?" Peaches pleaded.

"Okay, I'll do it, but don't be mad at me if I really put it down and hook them up"—she rolled her neck around—"and then your clients want to be my clients."

"Aww, girl, shut your mouth. And if you could steal them, then they were never mine," Peaches joked. "Make sure to lock up and I will see you early tomorrow," she said, kissing Janika on the cheek. "Thank you, Janika."

Peaches grabbed her jacket and almost flew out of her beauty shop. Her clients won't necessarily be pleased about her last-minute cancellations, but she knew that Janika would take care of them. Plus, she would rather hear a little fussing than miss out on a big come up.

Peaches arrived at the poker game ready to win. She was instructed to park in the back alley of a bail bonds business. She pulled behind the Porsche Panamera with dealer tags, took a look at her feminine features and long auburn tresses. She perfected her makeup and applied a coat of Mac lip gloss, then began to walk over to the back door of the building Tony, the guy hosting the game, used for his bondsman business. The spot was located in the 1200 block of Hull Street. Being a Church Hill girl, Peaches really didn't care too much for the south side of town, but she planned to get in, kick some ass, and get out.

She took the elevator to the ninth floor, walked down a narrow hall, and knocked on the brown door of what appeared to be an office. The door was opened by a petite man, who asked her the password for entry. Peaches obliged and walked into the dimly lit, smoked-filled room.

She arrived to see a group of men already sitting at the table. She pulled up a chair and sat among four other players at the table: a lawyer, the owner of a Porsche dealership, a bail bondsman, and the son of a well-known judge. The game was no-limit Texas Hold 'em and she decided to watch a few hands before she would ask to be dealt in.

Just as she joined the game, it was Tony's turn to deal. He was one of the city's most respected bail bondsman, among the thugs, dealers, and murderers, and it was a known fact that if someone committed a crime, Tony was the man to keep them from doing time while awaiting trial. At twenty-seven, the youngest of the four men, his parents had built the business and passed it over to him at the ripe age of twenty-five. In the past two years since Tony took over, business had tripled.

His mannerism and swagger were undeniable. Peaches could tell he had tons of women vying for his attention. His obnoxiousness seemed to come natural, not forced or contrived. Peaches could tell right away that, besides maybe his mother, Tony didn't respect women. He had no idea that his chauvinistic traits gave her an advantage from the moment she sat down.

Before dealing, Tony reached into the right pocket of his baggy jeans for a plastic sandwich bag, half-filled with white powder.

"Compliments of one trusty drug-dealing kingpin. This was my tip for not letting his ass make it to the bullpen," he bragged on how quick he got to the lockup to bail a client out.

He scooped a small amount of powder out with a card and dumped it on a black dinner plate. After taking a sniff up each nostril, he passed the plate around the table.

It wasn't hard for Peaches to figure out that the powder

was cocaine, because the guys had been cramming it up their noses all night. If it were an opiate, they would be nodding by now, not wide-eyed and fidgety.

Peaches lost count of how many times she had to kindly say, "No, thank you," when the plate of narcotic was pushed toward her. Besides staying focused, she had another reason for not sampling. Peaches didn't use drugs of any kind, for any reason. Her mother had been a dope head and overdosed at twenty-nine. A tragic thing like that either drove a kid to drugs or far away from them. For Peaches, it was the latter.

Mark sat to Tony's left, which made it his turn to bet first after Tony finally got the cards dealt. Mark was a genius when it came to convincing a jury that his client was innocent of a crime beyond a reasonable doubt, but was no more than average at hustling the cards. His trendy Ray-Ban sunglasses didn't throw Peaches off, because she had peeped his pattern. All night he predictably pretended to be weak when his hand was really strong, and strong when his hand was really weak.

After peeking at his cards for a full forty-five seconds, Mark bet seven hundred from the dwindling stack of C-notes and fifties in front into the center of the table.

Eric, fast and flashy like the cars he sold, said, "I call."

Peaches struggled to contain her smile. Eric was all flash and no substance. A behavior that Peaches had predicted might cost Eric a car title or two. And there were a couple of rides on his lot that she wouldn't mind having in her driveway.

Like the other three men at the table, Charles had been

losing all night as well. He took a quick look at his rags and quickly dumped them into a deadwood.

"I fold," he said, removing his Aviator sunglasses and placing them on the table, shaking his head, annoyed at the way the cards were flowing.

When the bet got to Peaches, without looking at her cards, she said, "I call the two . . . and bump it up another five grand." Then she tossed the money to the center of the table, to the rest of the players' chagrin.

Peaches may not have been able to physically read their minds, but their body language accurately conveyed it all to her; they were thinking: "The bitch can't be that good, can she?"

"Yup," she said out loud, smiling at her opponents. "I'm that good," she said, glad that they couldn't see her eyes dancing from behind her huge oversized Roberto Cavalli frames. "But there's only one way to find out," she taunted.

As testosterone overrode what little intellect they had, coke and the booze was left to make their decisions. It came as no surprise to her when all three vics still in the game called the raise. The pot was over eighteen thousand when Tony turned over the three-card flop. A deuce of hearts, three of diamonds, and ten of clubs, all mixed suited. She almost laughed out loud when each of their faces involuntarily clinched as if they'd just won a free colon exam. The shit was priceless.

Peaches wanted to get up and dance the Roger Rabbit dance, but she didn't. Instead, she kept her cool and displayed only a huge smile followed by a chuckle.

Beating these dudes was as easy as taking a four-inch filet mignon from a vegetarian; they were practically giving the money away. She almost felt bad for them, almost but not quite.

Nothing much changed as the night merged into morning. The only hands that she didn't win were the ones that she chose not to be in. Along with a couple of IOUs, she had won at least $75,000 worth of dead presidents that sat there in front of her staring at her, saying, "Peaches, Peaches, take me away." She decided that she would fulfill Jackson's, Grant's, and Franklin's wishes when she began filling her Louis tote with her winnings.

"I think I'm going to have to call it a night, fellas. I have to get up early for work in the morning."

The stares she got in return made her feel uneasy. "It's only one o'clock." Tony was the first to protest. He felt it was his obligation since he was hosting the game. He continued, "Don't tell me you're afraid that Lady Luck may leave before you do? Come on, let's play a few more hands," he practically begged.

Eric put the tip of a card into the dwindling mountain of coke on the plate and powered his nose. "Yeah, play a few more. Come on, Peaches," he said quickly as he went into his pocket and pulled out a stack of fifties and placed them on the table. "If you so sure that luck won't run away from you, then try your hand again," he said, licking his lips at her.

For a split second she wondered if that was his way of trying to convince her in a sexy way. She pretended like she didn't see the gesture, but then he did it again. This time he added an eyewink in with it.

The energy in the air was so awkward. It was at that very moment that Peaches regretted not bringing somebody with her. Being that they were all respected professionals, in a high-stakes game, she didn't think it was necessary. However, she quickly discovered that Tony was the type who didn't like it when things weren't going in his favor. He was the kid that when he lost, he took the ball and went home. *Too bad for him.*

"Luck is for suckers," she said with confidence and a smile as she continued to cram the money into her purse. "But if *she's* leaving, I don't mind giving her a ride," Peaches said with a slight chuckle, referring to Lady Luck.

Charles stole a glance at his watch. "I probably should be making my way to the crib, too, before my old lady changes the locks."

Eric downed a shot of Remy. "Stop being a pussy, Charles. How the fuck is a bitch that don't pay no bills or work in a pie shop going to lock a man out of his own house?"

"That's why I'm never getting tied down," Tony chimed in. "Too many badass bitches out here who can pay their own bills, live in and drive their own shit, ready and willing to jump through hoops for me, so why am I going to settle for just one of them. Ain't that right, Peaches?"

Besides the fact that the *bitch* word was being popped off a little too freely, Peaches didn't like the look behind Tony's red, glassy eyes after he removed his Gucci shades. She stood up, ready to break out of there. "I'll let you fellas work this one out on your own if you don't mind?"

Peaches couldn't get out of there and back across the water to her own stomping grounds on her side of town quick enough. "Will you get the door for me?"

"Depends," Tony said. He stared at her plump, heart-shaped behind like she wasn't wearing any clothes. "What you got for me?" he asked, then rephrased it. "I meant, what you going to do for me?"

Mark, Charles, and Eric started laughing. Then Tony must have lost his mind when he palmed her butt. With all her might, Peaches smacked his hand away and firmly said, "Don't do that."

Then this fool had the nerve to cup his crotch and say, "I know you want this dick, don't ya? Or you one of the bitches that prefer pussy?"

Peaches tried her best to remain calm. After all, this wasn't the first time that a stupid, disrespectful man, drunk or sober, thought he was God's gift to women. She locked eyes with him and was polite but absolute. "I may be a bitch, but I'm not a trick bitch. And definitely not your trick bitch either. Because it seems you've obviously got me confused. However, play-boy"—she looked him up and down, and rolled her neck a lit-tle—"I'm willing to overlook your mistake this one time. But like I said before, I'm ready to go. Now please unlock the door so I can be on my way."

Since Tony didn't take being put in his place too well, he paused, evaluating his next move, as if he were playing a poker hand. Then the fool went all in and snatched open her blouse. "Let me see what you working with."

He caught Peaches totally off guard and embarrassed. Her Victoria's Secret bra and all her cleavage were on full display for all of the men to view. Peaches just couldn't help her-self, she lost it. She angled her fist and cuffed, just like her father had taught her, and aimed for the part of the bone that she knew would impact him when she punched Tony in the face, right across his nose. She heard the bone in his nose crack under her tightly closed fist. Somehow—probably a combination of the alcohol and the coke—he managed to ignore the pain. Instead of backing up, like he should have, Tony picked her up like she was a feather and slammed her back-first on the poker table, bringing each guy's reflex to jump on their feet. With a forearm pressed over her neck, restricting her breathing and moving, Tony used his free hand to try to unfasten the belt to her tight-fitting True Religion jeans.

No amount of money was worth her getting beat up or raped for that matter. She knew that she was needed to get the fuck out of dodge before things went any further.

Though Peaches had won the money fair and square, she shouted, "You all can have the money back!" At that moment, she was trying anything to make amends so Tony would allow her to let it go, so she could leave.

Tony responded by applying more pressure on her neck, muting her words. "Shut the fuck up, bitch." The spit from his words almost landed in her right eye.

Desperately, Peaches's eyes dotted to each guy in the room, one after another, in search for help. But none of them had an ounce of compassion for her.

Eric yelled out, "Fuck that bitch, Tony! As a matter of fact, man, after you do her, I got dibs on that fat ass."

"Yeah, and I got front-row seating, voyeur style. I've always liked to watch," Mark slurred as he took a pull of a cigar.

"How you think that head is? I been needing a good blowjob, and those lips look like they can make my dick hum," Charles said. "Eric, you and I are going to have to flip for next."

Peaches knew she was doomed and basically shit out of luck. If she was going to be saved, she was going to have to save herself. None of them had an inkling of mercy for her, so she had to save herself however she could.

The Louis bag filled with the money was on the table next to her, the leather strap was still on her shoulder. Only by the grace of God, Peaches found a way to wiggle her hand inside the bag. No one even stopped her. "Bitch want to make amends. You can't buy your way back out of this," Eric said, his expression giving away his perverted plans.

They must have assumed that she was trying to give them the money back and continued to go back and forth about who would have her next.

Tony applied pressure with one hand and then let up a little with the other to focus his attention on his buddies. "Man, who want to make a side bet that I don't make this bitch scream in pleasure. Bet them ducats up, right now, niggas," he joked.

"That bitch knows she better take it like a champ," Eric said, looking at Peaches with a big smile.

That was the exact moment that her hand made it to the bottom of the purse. She dug her hand around her bag as Tony slid her jeans off her waist.

"I'm going to get her hot for you, Tee Man." Eric had the nerve to come over and begin sucking on her breast. Just as Tony was about to remove her pink thong underwear she found what she was searching for: the Glock 19 she had gotten from her father. Feeling the chrome handle felt like a present from heaven. She closed her eyes, and silently thanked the man above and asked for forgiveness all in the same breath.

Peaches didn't even bother to take the semiautomatic pistol from its resting place inside her purse. Instead, she just squeezed the trigger. And squeezed it again! Then again . . . and again . . . until the clip was empty!

2

Newsflash

Even for a city that once held the infamous nickname "murder capitol," the horrific crime that had been perpetrated earlier Saturday morning was nothing short of shocking. Two men dead from multiple gunshot wounds, a third and fourth critically injured, led all the morning news broadcasts. The fact that the victims were all very prominent citizens—one the son of a judge—fueled the already hot story to the brink of crazy media frenzy. The mayor scheduled a televised press statement for noon, three hours from now. But commander Toepani, an ex-military chief and now head of Richmond's SWAT team, planned to have the persons responsible for ruining his breakfast in his custody by lunchtime.

A tight Commander Toepani keyed the mic on his headset and asked, "Alpha and Charlie units, are you holding position?"

A resounding "Affirmative, sir," echoed back through his earpiece from the leaders of both three-man units. Their job was to make sure that the suspect didn't get out of the house without being apprehended. They wanted her alive but knew that she was armed and dangerous.

Toepani then gave the order to the remainder of his men. "We breach the doors on my command. . . ."

Inside of the house, a loud, shrill noise shattered the comfortable silence. Sitting at the kitchen table, Mickey jerked his head toward the ringing cordless phone. The poor man's nerves were shot to hell. He felt like he'd been running barefoot on razor-sharped blades ever since Peaches burst into the house at two in the morning, wearing mangled clothing, crying, talking about how she had murdered some men. At first he thought he was hallucinating or she was playing a trick on him, but the girl wasn't that evil to do something like that to him.

Peaches was Mickey's only daughter and only child. He never had interest in any kids. But after Emma's, the love of his life and Peaches's mother, fatal overdose, he raised her by himself the best he knew how. He'd had his own struggles with drugs, which he kicked the day Emma died, but he couldn't seem to shake off the lure of the streets. It wasn't always easy for Mickey being a single dad from the streets. Dragging around the little girl from drug houses to Narcotic Anonymous meetings, whorehouses, gambling joints to afterhours spots not only wasn't easy, but it also wasn't conventional. No one knew that better than Mickey, but he knew no one could protect her from the mean world like he could. He would have rather died and went to hell than to have been separated—by any length of time—from his little girl. Seven hours away from her while she was away at school was enough to make him miss her immensely, but he knew it was not only mandatory by law, but also the best thing for her . . . and being around other children would help her social skills.

In addition to making sure she was on top of her school-work, Mickey taught her every hustle and con he knew of, and persuaded his friends to school her on the ones he didn't know. But Mickey didn't educate his daughter from the school of hard knocks to be a predator; he did it so she'd never be anyone else's prey.

He knew that life could be extremely difficult for a kitten in a dog-eat-dog world. And if a cat didn't know the nature of the game, the ultimate cost could be life. It wasn't right in some people's eyes, but he never cared what others said. This was his child and she would be well rounded and wouldn't fall for the okey-doke.

The phone rang for the tenth time before Mickey finally answered it, "Hello?"

It was Nita, one of the neighbors from across the street.

"Hey, Mickey. Real quick, 'cause I know you busy. In case you didn't know, half of the damn Richmond police squad is outside of your house. I just wanted to make sure you and Peaches were okay. And they look like they coming to kill somebody and—"

He knew this woman could talk until the cows came home. Time was of the essence, so he cut her off, "I couldn't be better, under the circumstances," he exaggerated. "As for Peaches, she isn't here, but whenever I do talk to her, I will be sure to tell her that you called to check on her." Before hanging up, he added, "Thanks for the heads-up, sugar. I'll talk to you later."

Only half the force, huh? he thought as he shook his head and put the phone back on the hook.

Mickey had been expecting that much, plus some, ever since Peaches had filled him in with the gory details of the night before and all she'd been through. As far as he was concerned, a few dead cooked-up bastards was better than his daughter being gang-raped any day. The only problem was without any actual physical evidence, Peaches didn't stand a snowball's chance in hell of proving she was about to be raped. It would be her word against the reputation of men who were looked up to as model citizens in their city. And the fact that one was a judge's son, he knew his daughter would never get the opportunity to tell the truth to set her free.

Mickey prayed, wished, and pleaded with God that there was a way that he could somehow say that it was he who actually pulled the trigger. In a perfect world he would trade places with his daughter at the drop of a gavel.

But the world wasn't perfect, especially the one he lived in, but lucky for him he learned many moons ago to play the hands he was dealt.

"One."

Commander Toepani and his men were ready to enter his premises.

"Two."

Twelve men who made up his elite and special weapons

and tactical team all carried standard-issue M-16's, submachine guns, and wore standard-issue armor under their black windbreakers. They were trained for terrorist and hostage situations; but like most of their brethren all over the country, they were mostly used to raid the homes of drug dealers in the name of the "war on drugs."

"Three."

Battering rounds simultaneously knocked the front and back doors clean from their hinges. M-16's drawn, teams stormed up the interiors of the house in a manner that could be called controlled chaos.

Before Mickey or his nephew could finish their bowls of cereal, the members of the SWAT team aggressively barked out orders: "Get on the floor! Hands by your side! Lay down!"

With a gun to the back of his head, Mickey, acting as surprised as he knew how, asked, "What is this all about?"

"You know! Where is she?" Toepani asked.

"Where is who?" Mickey played dumbfounded.

"Peaches Alize Brown."

"She's not here. In fact, no one's here but me and my nephew." Mickey nodded toward the young boy lying on the floor to his right, which wasn't an easy task with his forehead planted firmly against the oak wood floors. "And for Christ's sake, take the guns off of the youngin'; he's only thirteen years old. You got the poor child scared shitless," he said, wanting them to lighten up on his nephew.

Three men from the team searched and secured the upstairs while the others continued checking the closets, under the sofas, anywhere else a person could attempt to hide downstairs while purposely knocking anything glass or breakable over by "mistake."

"And I see you people on the news saying you are trying to build a better rapport with the youth. This damn sure ain't no way to do it."

Commander Toepani told Corporal Hempstead, "Get Mickey and the boy to their feet."

Toepani gave Mickey a no-nonsense glare once he was standing. "It's real simple, you answer my questions truthfully or be charged with accessory after the fact to a double murder and a laundry list of other charges. Your fucking choice, man?"

Mickey stammered, "M-Murder?" as if he was taken totally by surprise.

"Where is your daughter? Peaches Brown, Peaches Alize Brown."

Mickey acted astonished that the commander would use Peaches's name and the word *murder* in the same breath. "What does Peaches haft to do with a murder?" He looked dumbfounded.

Toepani wasn't falling for it, he had seen it all before and he wasn't buying Mickey's act. If a father didn't know that his daughter wasn't alive and well, his first response should have been to the effect of, "Is my daughter okay?" Mickey taking the defense was all he needed to know. He was quiet for a second. "You can bet your ass we ain't gon' find her here. He'd be stupid to keep her here; she's probably long gone."

At that time, three SWAT officers who had been searching the upstairs came back down empty-handed. "All clear, Commander."

"I knew it," he nodded. Then Toepani addressed the nephew, "Hey, son. How you doing?"

The boy nodded his head with tears in his eyes.

"You got a name?"

The boy nodded his head a second time.

"Unless you are a mute or something, I would like to hear you say it."

"M-my . . . n-name . . . is . . . L-Lamont," the boy stuttered.

"Nice to meet you, Lamont. I want to ask you a couple of questions, okay?"

Lamont nodded.

Toepani tried to ease the boy's nerves a little. "How old are you, son?"

"T-th-thirteen."

Toepani cracked a smile. "I have a son your exact age. Tell me, Lamont, when is the last time you seen your cousin Peaches?"

Wearing baggy jeans, Air Jordans, a Philadelphia hooded sweatshirt, and fitted hat, Lamont looked to his uncle for help.

"Come on now," Mickey said to Toepani. "Now you interrogating a kid without his guardian's permission."

Commander Toepani pressed on. "You don't want to lie to me, Lamont. I'm here to help out."

"Not since yesterday morning, Friday," Lamont said.

"Enough of this bullshit," Mickey said. "You got my nephew shook up, and my sister is a reallll cuckoo bird, and she's one of those people always looking for a lawsuit. Now, I don't play about my Peaches, but she . . . now she's a real bitch and her kids are a whole other story. So that you don't waste more of the taxpayers' money, leave the kid and me alone."

Toepani thought about what Mickey had said, "We're wasting time. Let's get out of here. Take the father with us; we will question him further at the station and we will book him." The last part he thought would intimidate Mickey a little, but it didn't. "Call your momma, boy. I'm not going to take you downtown. You old enough to get home, right?" he said. "And remember the police are here to protect and serve." He patted Lamont on the back and exited out the house.

From beneath her "Lamont" disguise, Peaches watched the elite trained officers perp walk Mickey from the house in plastic flex-cuffs. She watched all the officers clear out.

She knew that they would try to pump him for information—information that he would never give—before they released him. Or eventually book him on a bogus charge of obstruction of justice. She took a deep, sympathetic breath due to the trouble she was putting her father through, having him hauled off to jail for her madness. Then she removed the fitted cap and the cutoff stocking that practically concealed her face by holding down and hiding her shoulder-length auburn hair.

Peaches cursed herself for wrapping the ace bandage so tightly around her breast that she could hardly breathe. But it had worked. It was impossible to tell that a set of 34Bs were being suffocated under the tight green Philadelphia Eagles sweatshirt she was wearing. She knew it was risky to unwrap herself, but she needed to breathe just for a second.

Over her dead body, she thought, would she ever turn herself in to the police and do even one day for killing that asshole who had tried to attack her. And for the others, she didn't give a flying fuck if they *all* had planned to join in or not. As far as she was concerned, rooting for the bastard, and doing nothing to stop it, made them just as guilty.

The burning question was, *What do I do now?* The answer: exactly what you and Mickey discussed, she talked back to herself. Get the hell out of Virginia until one of them could figure out a way to convince the authorities to believe the truth. *You better pack a lunch,* she told herself.

3

God Helps Those Who Help Themselves

Peaches exited the cab a few blocks away from the docks. What happened from here on out would determine her destiny. Mickey told Peaches that a man in a black hoodie would assist her. He would know who she was and that she was just to go to the dock in Hopewell and wait on the far east side. Even though it looked a little dangerous, she knew that her father would never steer her wrong.

She went to the designated spot and looked around for the person who was supposed to find her. The only problem was that all of the men were wearing navy and black hoodies at the docks. There were huge ships and vessels in the water by the dock. Peaches didn't have a clue why her dad would send her here. How would she escape Virginia by boat?

Still dressed as Lamont, her heart was pounding as she nervously stood by a ship on the east side until she heard noise come from over her shoulder. "Pssst, pssst." It startled her. "You Mickey's peoples?"

She was almost scared to answer the grungy-looking man. She had seen too many cop shows, and her emotions and imagination were running wild. Could it be the police on her trail? Had the person she was waiting for been made by the police and now this was an undercover? Then she took a deep breath and tried to get her mind right. Or was it the man her dad wanted her to meet with?

"Yes, Mickey sent me." She turned around to get a better look at the frail, older white man who only stood about five foot five with blond facial hair. He introduced himself, "I'm Frank, come on." He motioned and then started walking.

Peaches followed Frank through what seemed like a maze, passing various workers and countless boxes and freight in the shipyard. He walked her down to an area with huge cranes and big metal boxes the size of a two-level building. Peaches by now had figured out she would be riding with the man Frank to another city. However, he stopped before the boat she thought that they were heading to.

"This is where you will be staying. Get in here," he directed her, pointing to a cramped space in the front of a large metal box.

"In where?" she asked, dumbfounded. "It's dark in there," she said, glancing around, "and there is barely any room. Is there any air in that thing?"

Frank leaned in and looked her dead in the eyes. "Listen here, from what I understand you don't have no time to be asking no questions whatsoever. I'm only doing this 'cause

I owe Mickey a big favor. Now, this ain't first class I know, but there's no other way. If you go to any airport, bus terminal, or train station, you will be made. Do you understand? This is the only way out of the bear trap that they got set up for you. The choice is yours, but I advise you to jump in before they lift this cargo or you won't be able to make it on this shipment to Miami."

Peaches looked around, still unsure if she could trust Frank or if being locked in a hot metal box was a good idea.

He saw her thinking. "Now go on, get in now, gal. I'll come and check on you to see if you are okay. In the meantime, to try to pass a little time." He went in his pocket and passed her a pocketsize, handheld, battery-operated television that doubled as a radio.

She could not hide the uncertainty written on her face; although reluctant, she jumped in and he closed the heavy metal door. All she had was the dark and her thoughts to get her to Miami.

Soon after, Peaches felt the crane attaching to the box she was in, and seconds later, the box lifted with her inside and it dumped on to the boat. The noise rang her ears. She could hear commotion of all the workers giving directions, making sure the boxes were level. Peaches broke into a sweat. She was scared and fearful for her life when another box was placed on top of the one she was in. She wondered what she would do if her container collapsed from all the weight. But as she heard the squeaky noise of another container being placed beside hers, she knew there was nothing she could do—she was trapped in. There was no turning back.

If she made any noise or didn't calm herself down, she would be facing life behind bars; she had to take the chance of possibly being crushed.

How did her life get to this point? Mickey taught her everything she knew and he never prepared her how to run for her life; the problem was there was absolutely nowhere to run to.

Instead of driving herself crazy, all she could do was pray to God. He had saved her before and hopefully He would spare her again. Hopefully He would send someone to save her, like He had sent when she was seven years old when her mother was laying on top of her for two days dead.

She pulled out her headphones from her bag and tried to get a channel on the handheld television.

"Richmond's most brutal and baffling murder of this decade," is how the *Times Dispatch* described it, and the local news stations couldn't get enough of the story. Without fail, each time any of the networks recapped the horrific crime, they rolled footage from in front of Tony's bail bondsman business, cordoned by the all-so-familiar yellow police tape. Halfway through the segment, the image was replaced by a shot of Beauty Boutique and its owner—Peaches Brown— with the word SUSPECT prominent above the television screen. Out of all the cute pictures on her Facebook page that she had posted, they selected the worst. The not-so-attractive picture they used was one that someone had tagged her in.

Three days had passed since the ordeal, but with Peaches the images nesting in her head were still as vivid and graphic as the moment they'd happened. Like right now, she could still smell the liquor wafting from Tony's hot breath. Though she wanted so hard to block it out, she could feel his arm braced against her neck, the other pawing at the waist and button of her jeans. The noise wouldn't stop. She could still hear the others cheering him on. Eric calling for next, then Mark going back and forth about if he'd be next, like she was a new Porsche they were test driving. She could still see the wild, hedonistic glint in their eyes as she begged for help.

She, a helpless rabbit caught in their snare.

But the mirth quickly drained from their faces once the rabbit got her hands on the gun. Her father always said, it ain't never fun when the rabbit got the gun. The first shot, muffled by the inside of her purse, sounded like a firecracker. Her wrist barely jerked, the nine ejaculated the first bullet through the hole of the barrel, piercing the leather of the purse, then Tony's navel. Even right now, inside the eight feet by forty feet cold, dark, metal prison she'd been confined in for the past ten days, she could still smell the pungent odor of the gunpowder from the next fourteen shots that were fired.

When Tony was hit for the first time in the chest, he screamed out, "My God!"

Peaches whispered, "God helps those who help themselves," and continued to pull the trigger. Tony ate three more hollow points before meeting his God in person. Mark's fate was the same, and Eric's destiny was still unclear. As far as she knew, besides Peaches the only other person breathing after the smoke cleared was Charles, the judge's son, and he was on life support.

Being cooped up in an oversized metal shoe box was no

143

joke. She wasn't claustrophobic, at least not that she was aware of, but for some stupid reason the walls felt like they were closing in on her. Maybe it was a form of seasickness, she thought, before dropping down taking a seat on the uncomfortable sleeping pad.

The walls continued to inch in closer and she closed her eyes. She took a long, deep breath through her nose, and after mentally counting to twenty, she told herself, *It's going to be okay. God did not bring you this far to leave you.*

She exhaled through her mouth. *He leadeth me beside still water.* Then took in another one. *Yea, though I walk through the valley of the shadow of death.* A third time. *I will fear no evil because God is with me.*

By the fourth time, *It is He who will comfort me. God, not man, not anybody. God!* Filling her lungs with oxygen, she told herself, *God knows my heart.*

Saying the Twenty-Third Psalm over and over helped her cope, but it didn't change the fact that when she opened her eyes, the four walls stood still, but not the movie playing inside of her head. She knew it wasn't really a movie, just her thoughts, but physically she felt like she was watching a DVD—clear and vivid—chronicling her life. Oddly, the movie began at the present (her on the cargo ship hiding in the dark container) and from there it double-timed in reverse.

In a matter of seconds a year had gone by, and just like that she was twenty again. . . . A few more seconds, she was seventeen, going across the stage picking up her diploma. The pace of the reverse picked up and five more years were gone—she was twelve and it was her birthday. She could still see herself with Shirley Temple curls and makeup all over her face that she had novicely applied (but nobody could tell her that), leaning over the birthday cake and blowing out the candles, wishing her momma could be there with her; then it faded to black. When the next scene began, to her surprise and dismay, she was . . . seven.

Her birthday wish had come true, sort of in a twisted way. She was in the room of the small two-bedroom housing project that she lived in with her mother and her boyfriend Mickey. She was playing with a Rubik's Cube that she had gotten from a friend at school. Even as a kid she was always wise beyond her years and smarter than the majority of her peers. It didn't take long for her to make all the colors on all the sides match.

She was excited and knew that her mother would be proud of her. Her momma was in her bedroom with the door closed. Peaches knew that she was taking her feel-good medicine. Momma didn't like to do the medicine in front of her, but she'd seen it before. She'd seen Momma stick herself in the arm like they do at the hospital. Momma always felt better immediately afterward, just like at the hospital, except this one time—it sounded like Momma had slipped on something and had fallen down. She put her face through the door. "Is you okay, Momma?" But Momma didn't answer back. Not even to say what she usually would say, "Get away from the door and go play."

Her excitement turned to anxiety. Peaches didn't know why, or where it came from, but a voice told her to enter the room and check on her momma. First she didn't listen to the voice and said she wished her daddy was there, he would know what to do, but almost none of her wishes ever came true.

Momma once told her—the time she saw her crying because she hadn't gotten the pony she wished for—that wishes were only to be used for special occasions. That's it, that's all. Peaches didn't know what could've been more special than a pony, but Peaches didn't tell her momma that.

She called out to her "Momma" again and knocked on the door harder, and just like the first time, Momma didn't answer. Peaches was scared. She heard the voice again and it told her that Momma needed her help. The voice was coming from inside of her; she could feel it deep down in her stomach.

Even though it was going to cost her a spanking, Peaches listened to her gut, put her hand on the doorknob, and walked into the bedroom. Momma would probably be mad and fuss at her; she'd just have to tell Momma she felt it in her stomach and the voice told her to come in. It was strange because Momma didn't fuss at all. Instead, she laid there on the floor, her face frozen like a popsicle, with her medicine sticking out of her arm.

There was a knock on the door of her prison, which broke her thought. She wasn't expecting visitors, so she was silent and held her breath, praying to the man above that she had not been discovered.

"Are you okay?" Peaches exhaled after she recognized that it was Frank's voice, he was still her only ally right now. She hadn't even realized that she'd been holding her breath until then.

Inside the sealed metal cargo container, she answered, "I'm cool. How much longer?"

She was onboard *The Sea Voyager,* a privately owned humongous cargo freighter, illegally. Frank had given her a sleeping bag—which was more comfortable than the floor, but it barely kept the chill off during those first few nights—a case of bottled water, some fruit, a loaf of bread, and a pack of turkey, but she really didn't have much of an appetite anyway. She had left everything that could connect her to Virginia in Virginia, including her smartphone and iPad, which she really wished that she had to help pass the time. The only things she didn't abandon were an old duffle bag with a few articles of clothes and two hundred thousand in cash.

Frank said, "About eight more hours and we will be in the Port of Miami."

"Thank God," she said.

In return, Frank said, "God helps those who help themselves."

The six simple words chased chills up her spine, but she said under her breath, "Amen to that."

4

New Beginnings

Peaches felt a little uneasy as she was trying to blend in as she waited at a restaurant with outside seating on Biscayne Boulevard not far from the Port of Miami. People came and went and didn't even glance at her. They were either eating or talking with their lunch companion or chatting it up on their cellies. Peaches loved the fact that no one was paying any attention to her, and she kept trying to tell herself that fitting in here may be easier than she thought.

Miami was definitely a different vibe from the small city she was born and raised in. And after being cooped up in the metal box for ten days, fresh air was . . . so refreshing. After the grueling three-day journey, *The Sea Voyager* had finally docked at the Port of Miami. It took two and a half hours for the giant cranes to unload the cargo container she was in and another hour before Frank could get her out unseen and on her way.

The first thing she did after setting feet on dry land was find a pay phone, which was a harder task than anticipated, but when she did she called the number her father had given her. The man who answered asked if she had money and told her to catch a cab to this specific restaurant, and here she was waiting.

While she sat there with her eyes covered behind the big Gucci sunglasses, two police officers walked up, casing the place, as if they were looking for someone, maybe her, she thought to herself. She was about to get her duffle bag and purse and take off. As she was playing out the pros and cons in her head, if she should go or stay, one of the officers approached her. Her heart dropped; then he asked her, "Is someone using this chair?"

"It's yours," she said as she let on a slight, warm smile.

Checking her Michele watch, she was surprised by how quickly the time was passing now that she was off the barge. If her calculations were correct, she had about five more minutes before her ride would be there to pick her up. She was clueless as to what her benefactor would look like; all she was told was to look for a man with a salt and pepper beard behind the wheel of a black Ford pickup truck.

Hell, she thought, *that could be anybody.* She wished that she had gotten a better description of him, but he was supposed to be a friend of her father's. The stranger was from Mickey's past, whom up until this crisis had come about he'd never made mention of. Her father told her, "Just dial this number the moment you reach Miami and ask for Matteo."

Peaches had thought that she knew all of her father's friends. She and her father shared pretty much everything and, for the most part, there were no secrets between the two of them. Mickey entrusting her to a man she had never heard of seemed odd, but she knew her father must have trusted this man with his own life six times over to put hers in his hands. That alone was good enough for her.

Peaches looked up after she had placed the five-dollar tip on the table for the friendly waitress and saw a black Ford double-cab pickup truck. The lights on the truck flickered on and off three times. Peaches grabbed her duffle bag and headed toward the back passenger's side. When she was almost halfway to the truck, it crossed her mind that she wished she had more information on the driver of the ride. Especially when the passenger's side door opened and a man got out who didn't have a beard, and if he would've had one he was still be too young to have been gray. "Matteo?"

"Naw, lil' momma. I'm Sticks," said the sexy chocolate drop who stepped out of the truck. Peaches almost melted on the spot, embarrassed to be meeting such a handsome man after being locked up in a crate for days. She'd had better days. She was about to turn around when the Sticks guy said, "Matteo's right there." He gestured with a nod making it known that Matteo was the driver.

Just then, an older man leaned forward. "Come on, pretty girl, hop on up in here." Then he spoke to Sticks, "Junior, act like you got some home training and help the girl with her bags." He put the truck in Park. "The lady been waiting long enough because you couldn't decide what sneakers to put on."

Peaches glanced down to take a peek at what kind of tennis shoes Sticks had on, but the irony of it was he didn't have any on. He sported a pair of Air Jordan flip-flops with snow-white, fresh out of the pack ankle socks.

Matteo peeped her checking out his son's footwear and said, "He's always holding me up, just like he's doing me now. I was going to leave him, so he decided to do the Miami thing and slip his slippers on and bring his black ass on."

"A'ight, Pops, I got this covered," Sticks said to his dad while relieving Peaches of the weight of her duffle bag she was carrying.

"That's all you got?"

"Besides my purse. I'm traveling light, on the account that I was in a real hurry when I left."

When Sticks smiled he had a beautiful set of white teeth that complemented his dark chocolate smooth skin. "But what do you have in here? Bricks?" he asked.

"Junior, you lift all those weights, I know you not complaining," Matteo said, overseeing everything.

Peaches couldn't help but notice his nice physique; his muscles were poking out in a nice way from under his crisp, brand-new white T-shirt.

After placing her bags in the bed of the truck, he took her hand, helping her into the front seat. He then slid into the back seat of the cab.

Peaches felt a little uncomfortable being in the car with two strange men who she didn't know and had never met before in a city she knew nothing about. The fact that she was riding shotgun with someone sitting right behind her only intensified the uneasiness she felt even more. As a young girl, Mickey had taught her to never let anybody whom she didn't trust sit behind her in the car. Plenty of supposed to be street dudes who had violated that rule of thumb died by a shot to the back of the head or being suffocated to death.

The two men seemed to be nice folks and she knew her father would never put her in harm's way. So, she just chalked it up to them being gentlemen and allowing her to sit in the front seat.

"Girl," Matteo said, glancing up over at her. "If you ain't the spitting image of yo momma."

Shocked by his comment, Peaches replied, "I didn't know that you knew my mother." It was a compliment that Peaches had heard before. "Everybody says that."

"Heck yeah, I knew your mother. We all go way back." Matteo sort of glassed over as if he was reminiscing about something. "Me, Mickey, and your momma. Boy, we dug Richmond a new asshole back in the day. Those were some good times." He smiled as he focused on the road.

Peaches smiled. She wanted to ask about those good times, because she mostly heard dark things about Emma. She looked over at Sticks, and he seemed lost in dark thoughts. She wondered why he didn't share his father's sentiments about the old days back in Virginia. Had he known her mother? As much as she wanted to know, she didn't think this was the right time or place to be caught in her memories and feelings about her mother. She had much more current issues that needed all of her focus right now, so she decided that she would save those questions for Matteo later. Matteo made small talk the entire drive, until they finally came to a stop in front of a nice size house in a neighborhood called Weston Hills.

Matteo and his son set her on the top floor of their home. Her temporary home was their fully finished attic that had been converted into a bedroom suite. Matteo said, "This room is yours for as long as you need. Make yourself comfortable, so feel free to have the run of the house."

Sticks dropped her duffle bag on the oversized brown and black zebra print chair. He didn't seem as friendly as he was when they first met. Peaches said, "Thank you," to them both.

"I'm going to have Junior show you the rest of the house and a few of the amenities you will need to know. If you need anything, just let me know and I'll get it for you. I want you to feel right at home here."

She nodded "okay" but wasn't sure that she could ever feel at home in a strange city, having to always look over her shoulders, especially under the current circumstances, but she would have to make do.

"Towels and such are in the closet in your bathroom over there," Matteo pointed out. "I'm not sure what you drink or like to eat, but make a list and Junior, he will get it for you." Matteo was going out of his way to make sure that she felt at home.

"Okay, thank you," she said. "I will try not to be too much bother."

"Don't be silly, pretty girl. You ain't no bother at all. In fact, it'll be nice to have a woman around the house," he said with a wholesome smile, then changed the subject. "Your father said you were a master artist and was good at changing your appearance."

"Yes, sir," Peaches nodded. "I'm pretty good with makeup," she said modestly.

"Well, the things you need for that, make a list and send Junior for it. And he will show you where to keep those things at." He lowered his voice. "I have a special hidden place for all of those things right over there." He pointed to a mirrored wall.

She redirected her attention and Sticks walked over to it. He did something with the light switch, then grabbed the remote to the television and the wall opened. She couldn't believe her eyes; it was like something off of television.

"Oh, wow." She was definitely surprised. "No one would ever know about this."

"That's the idea," Matteo said with a smile, proud of his secret compartment.

It was a small room, but it had everything in it one needed to survive for a few days. There was a full-size bed, a small dresser, a small bathroom over to the right. There was a television, a radio, a laptop, a small refrigerator, microwave, a set of dishes, along with some perishables.

"This is where you will retreat just in case the police comes here or anything of that nature."

"Okay," she nodded. "I can't thank you enough."

"No need to thank me. Your father is a very good man and he loves you with all his heart." He thought for a second and then shared, "Once he helped my son out of a real complicated jam and never breathed a word of it to a soul. That's the type of thing that people like me never forget. Though we could never repay him, the least I can do is keep you safe and free. And as long as you are under my watch, that's what I intend to do, or like that rapper boy say, die trying."

She smiled. "Mr.—"

He cut her off, "It's Matteo, no need for the formal misters and all that kind of stuff. We are family, my dear."

"Sorry, it's out of respect. But as I was saying, I simply can't express to you my appreciation," Peaches said, but couldn't help but let her mind wander off to what were the circumstances around Mickey helping Sticks. But her thoughts were quickly interrupted.

"Oh, before I forget to tell you, I have this doctor flying in from the Dominican to do a minor little procedure to alter your fingertips," said Matteo.

"Really?" That one caught Peaches off guard. She hadn't really heard of such a thing, nor had she known that there was a way that one could alter their fingerprints. She couldn't believe that this was her life at this moment. It was almost like irony; for years makeup and imaging had been her passion, and now it was going to be one of her key ways of survival.

"I didn't know anything like that was possible." She asked, "Does it hurt?"

Matteo obviously sensed her apprehension. He scratched the side of his head, exaggerating deep thought, before saying, "I heard that it's slightly painful for few minutes after." Then he smiled. "But it's better than the old way?"

The smile was assuring, but Peaches had to ask, "I'm almost afraid to hear, but I have to know. What was the old way?"

"To dip the tip of your fingers in acid. And trust me"—he looked at her—"it burnt like the dickens."

Peaches looked into his eyes trying to figure out whether he was joking or not. Matteo would have made a good poker player because he was almost impossible to read.

"You are joking, aren't you?" But there was something about Matteo that told her that he didn't go around making up things.

"As I was saying," he said, ignoring her question, not wanting the poor child to be scared shitless at something that she would have to get done. To lighten the mood, Matteo changed the conversation. "As I was saying, I don't want you to hesitate about making yourself at home. Whatever is ours . . . is yours. If it's something you want that's not here, don't hesitate to let either of us know. You hear me?"

Matteo was so hospitable and gracious, the only thing that Peaches could say was, "Thank you. To the both of you."

Then came the conditions. Matteo said, "Now the only thing I ask of you . . ." At that moment Peaches knew it was too good to be true, but she listened to what he had to say. He looked in her eyes and said firmly, "Under no circumstances do I want you to leave this house or go anywhere unaccompanied by either me or Junior." He put his finger up, and added, "At least until we know for sure that it's cool to do so. I promised Mickey that I'd watch your back."

"Okay," she said with no complaint. Even if she did, she wasn't in any position to do so. Besides, Lord knows she needed somebody to have her back.

5

Ocean Drive Strip

In those first days, Peaches tried to get a read on her hosts and the lay of the land. In many ways, Matteo was just like her father, and when he wasn't busy handling business, he reminisced with her about his days back in Virginia. But he didn't mention her mother again after Sticks walked out during one of his stories.

Sticks seemed to run hot and cold. Sometimes Peaches would catch him looking at her—like when she was sunbathing on the deck—and she knew he was undressing her with his eyes. But whenever Peaches tried to talk to him, he seemed polite but dismissive. He finally came around when she asked to ride along with him to get acquainted with the Miami streets. After all, it was her new home until her father could figure out a way to clear her name.

After a few days of being stuck in the house or rolling with Sticks while he towed cars or ran one of the other family businesses, the Dominican doctor finally arrived in Miami to alter her fingerprints. The procedure—done with a laser—

went fine, but Peaches couldn't help feeling low-spirited. She couldn't call anyone back home, didn't know if her father was okay. The reality of it all was hitting her like a bag of hammers. She would never be able to return home again until she was proved innocent.

Peaches worried that she may never be able to prove that she committed the homicides in self-defense. How would she be able to live life on the run, and for forever? And the answer was yes if the alternative meant life in prison. She had no choice but to try to pick up the pieces and press on, always looking over her shoulder and sleeping with one eye open and one eye ready to open at a moment's notice.

She was forced to seek refuge in a new city. She would have to learn the people, areas, and culture, and she didn't know anyone; everything and everyone was a mystery to her. In all actuality, the beautiful side of Miami wasn't such a bad place to start over.

A couple of days later, as an attempt to cheer her up, Sticks took her out to lunch. It was her first time on South Beach. She had heard a lot of chatter about it but had no idea that she would love it so much on the happening Ocean Drive strip. On one side of the street, the crystal-colored sand and jade blue water looked like a slice of paradise on Earth. The Eves strutting their stuff half naked, while the Adams fantasized about biting the proverbial apple. The other side of the street was lined with restaurant after restaurant serving every dish and delicacy imaginable.

It was barely noon on a Sunday and the strip was jam-packed, everyone enjoying God's gift that had been embellished by the hands of man. But even with all the excitement,

Peaches couldn't escape the possible thought that prison could be in her future. In the midst of all the excitement of watching the fast cars and faster women, the what-ifs clouded Peaches's thoughts. What if she was caught and dragged back to Richmond to trial? What if the jury didn't believe her and she was found guilty? What if she had to spend her life in jail for protecting herself? What would she do in jail but rot and die? One murder meant life in prison, but four, that was a guaranteed four life sentences, and add on a few attempted murders and that equaled forever. Peaches could not even imagine ever allowing that to happen.

Sticks could tell that her body was there with him, but her mind was on the other side of the would-haves, could-haves, and should-haves with the ifs, ands, and buts in Virginia. Though she tried to keep a poker face, he somehow could read her mind.

"You know you should take advantage," Sticks said, his sexy dimples distracting her from her pretense of watching the people who passed by.

Peaches turned her attention to Sticks. "Advantage of what?" she asked.

He reached across the table and clasped her hands. "Look, baby girl." He never used her real name in public, not wanting the wrong person to hear it slip out. "With so many ethnicities, Miami is truly the world's melting pot. This is the perfect opportunity to blend in and be whoever you want to be." Sticks leaned in close to her ear and spoke to her in a tone above a whisper. "You will be one of maybe millions of people who choose to start a new life here, in a land of new beginning, for so many."

"I hear you." She spoke slowly, trying to figure out if he was talking about her or something more.

"Real talk, baby girl. People risk their lives to come here on old inner tubes, rafts, and planks of wood just for the sake to live a better life and to escape the hell where they came from. You should do the same."

The things Sticks said definitely made good sense—a lot of sense. She looked down at their joined hands and felt butterflies of excitement in her stomach. Yes, she could re-create herself in Miami, and she could see herself giving Sticks a test drive.

Once Sticks felt he had her attention he pushed even harder to take his point home. He looked in her eyes and kept going on. "It would be so simple, easier than you think, probably. Your Pops told mine amongst your many talents that you create images for people all the time. Gotta give you props, that's a pretty neat gift to have. And right now, that's the best thing going for you. So if you can do for other people, you can definitely do that shit for yourself."

She listened and took in every word he was saying, and he knew he had her, so he kept going. "Think about whoever you aspire to be and be her. Or him for all I know."

Peaches slugged him on the shoulder. "You are not funny." She play hit him.

"I'm serious, and Pops will get the proper papers for you. Birth certificate, social security number and card. Trust me, that type of shit is right down his alley. He knows people who could 'paper' you up and make you legit. And whatever you need to create this person on a physical level, I'll

assist you however you need me to. So don't worry, just figure it out and we got ya back."

Peaches looked in his eyes and saw how genuine he truly
was. Besides her father, and his friends, nobody wanted to
make sure that she was really okay. She was flattered that
Sticks really wanted the best for her.

Peaches joked, "But be careful who and what you ask for.
What if I create someone neither one of us like?" She said
sarcastically, "You may be helping me create a monster like
Dr. Jekyll and Mr. Hyde."

"I'll take my chances," he said with a lopsided smile. "And
I think you are far too pretty, outside and inside, to turn into
any type of monster. One more question."

"Shoot."

"Have you thought of a name yet?"

She hadn't, but right then one rolled off her tongue and
it sounded perfect . . .

"Lolah Escarda."

6

Lolah Escarda

The process of creating her new persona began by removing her current weave and dying her auburn hair to jet black now. She settled upon a bob haircut with some Chinese bangs. The job on her hair alone had taken the entire rest of the day.

The next morning she was up early, ready to go shopping for her new gear to complement the look she had created. Before leaving the house, she inserted some hazel contacts into her eyes. With her pecan complexion it totally blended in perfectly, giving her an exotic appearance; she could easily pass for Dominican, Haitian, Trinidadian, or Ethiopian, or someone of Spanish decent.

Between Aventura Mall and the Bal Harbour Shops, she blew through a ridiculous amount of money all in the name of re-creating herself. She knew her new persona appreciated nice things and designer tags.

She looked at herself in the mirror wearing one of the new outfits, new hair color and style, contacts, and makeup. Lolah

Escarda stared back: a beautiful, young, sexy, and sophisticated woman. At that moment she realized that not only was she totally morphing into someone else, but long gone was the sweet, innocent, urban girl who had arrived from Virginia on a barge a little over two weeks ago. Everything she purchased was more sexy, sophisticated, and high end than any of the things she owned in Virginia. Her entire style would be different from her hip-hop persona that she fled.

Sticks had changed too. It seemed like since they'd had their conversation at the restaurant on Ocean Drive, Sticks was trying to put his stamp on her. She was definitely interested, but she didn't want him to get the idea they were exclusive.

Creating Lolah required the kind of shopping that was an all-day affair and Sticks had been a good sport about it.

It was dark when she tried on one last dress. When she came out, she looked at herself in the triple-take mirror in the luxury boutique shop.

Sticks, patiently waiting with all of her bags, looked up from his iPhone with a nod and a look of approval. "That one looks like it was made for you, baby girl." He was about to say something else but just that quick Lolah had already caught the attention of another admirer.

"That is everything. Oooh, honey child, baby, baby, baby. And I say that in my Wendy Williams voice." This flamboyant "shim" walked up wearing some skintight red skinny leg jeans with a neon pink sheer button-down shirt—nipples showing and all. Some red, white, and black bracelets and big red and gold earrings. Lolah looked him over and saw his high-heeled animal print Christian Louboutin pumps, and his big limited edition Louis Vuitton bag holding a couple of tops in his hand. He had his hand covering his mouth. "Ooohhh, you looking kind of scrumptious there, honey dip."

"Why, thank you, and you looking kind of brightly couture yourself."

"Well, thank you, my dear," he said, batting his eyelashes. "You not slouching yourself, honey; you give me fever with that dress on. Somebody going to be real lucky," he said, putting his hand up to his mouth as if it was a secret.

"Aww, that's sweet," Lolah said, as the two of them could've continued exchanging compliments all day.

"And who did your makeup?" he asked.

"I did."

"Shut up," he said. Then asked, "You a makeup artist?"

Lolah looked at Sticks as if she wanted to say yes, but let him know that she knew better when she said, "No, but I love to play in makeup."

The saleslady came with a top, but Lolah shook her head and declined it.

"What else are you trying on?" the guy asked. Lolah showed him the other things and they chitchatted like two old friends while Sticks was sending texts as if he were not paying the two any mind. Lolah asked the saleslady to unzip her and she went back into the dressing room.

The cross-dressed guy was impressed. "Where are you going? Where are you thinking about wearing that dress to?" he asked from the other side of the door.

Sticks spoke up. "Nowhere special, this is just her life."

"Oh, okay, WOW. What a life Ms. Thing has." He peeked

out the door. When Lolah opened the door to exit her fitting room, he looked her over and said, "We need to be friends. It's simply a must."

Lolah smiled in agreement, then said, "Yes, we do. It's a must."

"I'm Lyle," he introduced himself.

"And I'm Lolah."

While the two exchanged phone numbers, Sticks paid for the last two dresses and grabbed the bags from the saleswoman. Lolah liked how Sticks handled everything throughout the entire day. He was always a perfect gentleman and treated her like a queen. From the way he looked at her, she knew he wanted more than friendship. Peaches was still feeling him out, but knew something had to give soon 'cause there were so many things, and women, he could be doing instead of spending his time with her. But so far, there were no strings attached.

7

Beat It

"Girl, you know the new Louis just came in, and you know we needs to be up in there," Lyle said to Lolah.

"Without a doubt." Lolah was excited. That's the one thing that she was able to keep from her past, her admiration for Louis Vuitton. "I'm gonna let you know what time I can meet you there."

"Actually, baby cakes, I need you to come scoop me up and we ride together." Lyle often spoke of himself in the third person. "The Bombshell is having a little car trouble. And over my dead body will I let something as small as an automobile keep The Bombshell away from anything limited edition."

"Yes, I know The Bombshell is entirely too exclusive for that," Lolah acknowledged. "Well, let me try to pull a rabbit out of my hat. I'm going to call you back in a few."

Lolah hung up the phone wondering how she was getting

out of the house without one of her two permanent chaperones in her space.

It had been two months since she had settled into her new Miami life, and without a doubt, it was time she broke loose on her own and made a life for herself. The only problem that she faced was that she had to convince Matteo to let his guard down a little. She wanted her own car, to be able to come and go as she pleased, and most of all to move around without Sticks on her heels.

But she had to admit that she secretly liked Sticks doting over her. He was tall, dark, and hella handsome. Though he was a tough guy in so many ways, in the most important ways, when it came to her, he was a perfect gentleman. He was naturally a fun guy to be around, and a man around town. He knew everybody in the city and was good company, but she knew she couldn't build her new beginning around him. Besides, he had his own life to live. Just because hers had been disrupted didn't give her the right to intrude on his.

She wanted and needed to break away. She felt like she was being too sheltered, and even though Sticks didn't show it, she was sure that he was tired of babysitting her. So before things went and she wore out his welcome cramming his style, she wanted to begin to build her own life.

Lolah approached Matteo, who was sitting in the kitchen reading *The New York Times* while watching the news at the same time. Go figure.

He said, "Good morning, beautiful," when she leaned in, kissing him on the cheek.

"Good morning," she said. "Would you like a cappuccino?"

"Don't mind if I do," he said with a smile as she put the high-end coffeemaker on. She got the cups out, popped two fresh bagels in the toaster, and sat down across from him.

"So, I want to thank you for everything that you've done for me. I mean, the way that without any questions you two bachelors let me move into your house, never complaining about all of my stuff. You two have made my needs and my survival a priority just on the strength of my daddy and I appreciate that."

"That's because you are special and you are our priority," Matteo confessed to her.

Her heart almost melted. "Aww, thank you," she replied, while wondering who was buttering up whom now. She got up and grabbed the bagel and put the cream cheese spread all over it for him. Then she came out with it. "Matteo, I think it's time that I did a few things alone."

"Really? Things like what?" he asked, with one eyebrow raised.

"Like . . . girl stuff."

"Such as?" He questioned her as if she were his very own daughter, which was something he never had. But having Lolah around made him like the idea of it. But at his age, he'd passed on trying to bring that thought into reality. Embracing and treating Lolah like she was his own was going to have to do.

"Like . . ." she said, seeking direct eye-to-eye contact. Her dad used to tell her that if she wanted a man's respect, she should always look him in the eyes when speaking to him. "Go to the mall and have lunch with a friend."

"You do that now," Matteo said, referring to the times when he or Sticks escorted her.

"Aww, don't get me wrong, Sticks is the best and he really holds me down and looks out for me. But at the end of the day, I'm such a girly girl and he's such a man's man. And in his defense, he doesn't want to be hanging around at the mall all day with me. He got things to do and people to see."

"Now, don't get it wrong. He likes the mall too. That boy of mine is serious about his clothes," Matteo said. "Serious."

He wasn't exaggerating either; Sticks did do the damn thing with the gear whenever he changed out of his towing uniform.

"He is," she had to admit. "But not the same way as a girl."

Matteo was quiet for a minute, but he understood where she was coming from. He just hated that it came this soon. He knew good and well that he couldn't continue to smother the girl, and if she truly was going to be Lolah Escarda, he would eventually have to let her fly. "I can loosen the reins a little, but there will still be rules and a curfew," he finally said.

"I will still stay close to home and under Sticks still, but I just want a little freedom."

"I understand. But while you are roaming the city alone, just don't forget why you are really living here. I think you have to make a life for yourself, but you must be very careful. You never know who is watching you or what little thing can open a can of worms," he lectured.

"Understood," she said with great sincerity and respect.

Matteo gave her the keys to a black BMW Z4 roadster and ushered her into the garage where the car was parked.

"Very nice!" He showed her how to work some of the added amenities. She was surprised that he would give her a car this nice.

"Yeah, not too flashy, a nice vehicle for this Lolah girl. I know you have to look the part. You can't have eight hundred dollar shoes on and be driving a thirty thousand dollar car. Just doesn't make sense," he reasoned. "I'm not too old to know that image is everything."

Lolah smiled because truly it was.

"And perception is key," she added.

Matteo was a wise man with great understanding. Though he was a bit old-fashioned sometimes, she loved him like an uncle, godfather, or even a surrogate father for how he had taken her in. Though he could never in a million years take the place of her real father, he was a damn good fill-in.

It was still uncertain to her the true dynamics of the bond that tied Matteo and her father together. But one thing she was sure of, it was a strong bond. And as bad as she wanted to know, she couldn't take time to figure it out. Instead, she hurried, got dressed, and rushed out the house before he changed his mind.

Though he could never be too careful when it came to Peaches, when things calmed down a bit, Mickey got a burner phone to call Peaches. Even though he'd been pulling in favors around town, trying to dig up dirt on the men Peaches killed, he didn't have enough ammo for her defense. Toepani and his cops were determined to find Peaches, and posters were up all over town offering a reward for her capture. Months had passed, and it looked like Peaches was going to have to stay in hiding for a lot longer than expected.

Once they were done with the call, Mickey would destroy the SIM card and the phone so the call would not be tracked. For each call, Mickey got a new phone from a different spot. Mickey usually called Peaches every Thursday to check on her and give her an update on the investigation.

After Peaches spoke with her father, she went to pick Lyle up from his house, and they had a great day hanging out together. He was as extra as they come, and exciting at the same time. Being out with him made her realize just how much she'd missed her girlfriends and the ladies from her salon back home.

Lolah and Lyle cruised down Washington Street with the top back and Chanel scarfs wrapped around their heads, tied under their necks, Thelma and Louise style. Lyle turned the volume down on the classic Lil' Kim, Queen B CD they were rocking. "Can you pull in here and let me run into the store?" Lyle asked. "Chile', you don't even have to park. You can sit in the car; I just need to pick up one thing. I'll be in and out in a flash, trust," he assured her.

"Cool," Lolah said as she pulled in front of the high-end couture boutique.

Parking was damn near impossible to find, so she pulled right in front of the store in the no parking zone, flipped on the emergency flashers, and prayed that no one came to give her a ticket.

Lyle hopped out and made his way in while Lolah continued listening to the music but didn't crank the volume back up. While she waited for Lyle to come back, naturally, she pulled the mirror down on the sun visor and applied a layer of Lucid lip gloss to her kissers and Mac press powder on her face to take the shine off her forehead. As she put the finishing touches on her face, something told her to look in the rearview mirror. Lyle was hightailing it out of the store, working his six-inch stilettos in the wind like track shoes. He was moving pretty fast, but not fast enough. It seemed like he wanted to run, but his six-inch stilettos were holding him up.

"Start the car, bitch," he managed to yell as he almost fell. He ran his out of his shoes and left them suckers right on the ground. She saw the look on his face that said, "Time to break out, bitch." And make no mistake about it, she didn't hesitate to do what she was told to do. Whatever was going on, she didn't want to be caught up in the mix.

Without hesitation, she put the car in Reverse, hit the button to raise the top, and backed up a little to try to help him get to the car quicker. When he noticed that Lolah was bout it-bout it, that's when Lyle turned around and, like a track star, made a dash to go back and grab his shoes.

Unbelievable. "Are you fucking kidding me?" she said as if he could really hear her.

Lolah had one foot on the gas and one on the brake. She was about to reach over for the door handle, but he dove into the car without even opening the door as it was rolling down the street. One of the store employees had been hot on his heels literally hitting the trunk of the car as Lolah took off like a madwoman. The BMW ate up Washington Street and hung a right on Fifth.

Lolah didn't know what the hell was going on, but she didn't waste time asking questions.

"What the fucccckkkk just happened?" Lolah asked as she peeled out of there and headed northbound on the highway, making a clean getaway.

"Bitch, I almost lost these motherfuckers?" Lyle had taken off his crystalized Yves Saint Laurent pumps off and held them in his hand, examining them for scratches or scuffs. "Boo-Boo, do you know what I had to do to get these bitches?" Before Lolah could respond, Lyle told her, "These babies were supposed to be on back order, but I hunted these babies down like wild game. Shiiiiit, I wish I would let these gems get away." Lyle kept going on about the damn shoes while Lolah was in the process of trying to remember everything that Matteo had told her just this morning about the tricked-out BMW. She hit a button on the CD player to change the license plates. Another button to make the transitional tint on the windows to get darker. And another to change the inside color of the wheels from black to chrome.

"Bitch, what the fuck we rolling in?" Lyle was surprised at the car's features. "A fucking James Bond 007? Bitch, you got some explaining to do about this pimped-out shit. I know your peoples do cars and shit, but this shit here . . . is some atomic bomb type shit."

Lolah ignored him and said, "Shut the fuck up about the car and the got-damn shoes, and tell me why in the hell the people was chasing you like you stole something."

"Some fucking bullshit," Lyle said, blowing her off. He then reached into his Chanel bag for his phone and called up somebody.

Before Lolah could begin to express her frustrations, he was already jabbering a hundred miles a minute to someone on the other end of the phone. "Why the fuck? You give me a hot-ass card?" he said to whomever he was on the phone with. "Yeah, that shit was fucking flagged like a soldier. Hell, like a fool wearing a turban in the got-damn airport. Motherfuckers got The Bombshell on tape and some more shit. Hell, fucking with y'all, I might be on the evening news tonight. Who the fuck knows? All the fuck I do know is they almost had The Bombshell's ass, but I smelt something fishy by the way the cashier was acting. Bitch gone tell me she gotta call in for an authorization." He continued with the one-sided conversation. "After the shit took too long to go through, the bitch tells me something going on with their machine. But The Bombshell is smarter than that. I knew that look, and The Bombshell immediately said I'd come back. And as soon as I made my way to the door, bitch motioned for security to grab The Bombshell. But shit, The Bombshell was too fast for that fat motherfucker who luckily was paying for his Chinese food he'd just ordered."

Lolah had heard more than she needed to hear and was furious. Her first thought was to smack the cowboy shit out of him so hard that his head would fly out the passenger's side of the window. But she knew that it was best that her intellect override her emotions, and that's when she took a deep breath and asked him to get off the phone.

"Hang up," Lolah said to Lyle, then took an exit off the highway.

Lyle wasn't done with making his point on the horn and had the unmitigated gall to put his index finger up, for *her* to wait a minute while he finished *his* one-sided conversation.

Lolah slammed on the B'mer's brakes, forcing the tires to produce skid marks. Lyle bumped his head on the dashboard. Lolah said, "Now get the fuck off the phone." She spoke firmly in a way that Lyle knew she was serious as cancer. He didn't say the proper good-bye to whomever he had been going on and on with. He simply disconnected the call.

Lolah was trying to keep her cool, but cool went out the window a few miles back. "Now, let me get this straight. So, you went into a store, leaving me out front of the store, top back, music playing, in freaking bird's-eye surveillance camera's view, unbeknown to me that I'd been given the title as getaway driver?" she asked, wanting an answer from Lyle even though she already knew what the answer was.

"I mean . . ." He looked for words. "I didn't think it was going to be no big deal." Lyle shrugged his shoulders and in a carefree way said, "Darling, you are making your makeup crack. A frown is not good for your look, honey," he said and then got back to the topic at hand. "Seriously, Ms. Thing, my plan was to be in and out. Wanted to get this fire-ass blazer that I had to have. And I had even picked you up a little designer dress and was going to surprise you with it."

Lolah was stunned into silence, quiet as a church mouse, letting her mind run on how serious this shit really could be. Something as petty as some bullshit ass blazer could get her tore off and thrown into jail for the rest of her life.

Lyle was oblivious. "Honey, you just don't understand, that shit, that would have given the haters diarrhea. It was just that spicy."

Meanwhile, Lolah wasn't hearing anything he had to say at this point.

"Honey pie, get out the middle of this damn street and stop playing."

She looked him dead in the eyes and firmly said, "Get the fuccccckkkkk out of my shit."

Lyle had seen the look in her eyes that conveyed to him it was best to act like he was living out a Michael Jackson song and "Beat It" while he still could.

8

The Bootlegs

After putting Lyle's hot ass out of her car, Lolah drove a few more blocks away, parked the B'mer, and checked her lip gloss in the mirror. Once she was sure no one was looking, she gathered her personal things and got out too. She popped the trunk, grabbed her booty bag out of it, and stuffed it with the rest of the contents and let Pat and Turner go to work, patting the pavement and turning the corner.

She couldn't do it quick enough. There was a good chance that someone had seen what happened and gotten a good look at the car. Who knows? The salesman who was hot on his trail or someone else who was watching the whole thing unfold could have jotted the license plate number down. The very last thing she needed was to be stopped by the Jakes. Sticks told her that the ID Matteo had gotten for her was official and it looked legit, but Lolah wasn't in a hurry to put the documents to any kind of unnecessary tests. Especially not for some stupid-ass guy who wanted a blazer.

Once she had bent and turned a few corners, the first

thing she did was call Sticks. "I'm in trouble," she said when she got him on the phone, no *Hello, how are you?* Just those three words and he was all ears.

Since the call had come in from her cell, Sticks knew she wasn't in jail. He quickly asked where she was, but before she could answer the first question, he fired off another. "Are you hurt?"

Lolah could hear the concern in his voice and it was genuine. She wondered if he was this way with everyone.

"It's nothing like that." Too embarrassed to even give him the rundown over the phone. Her trying to form the words in her mind, before speaking, the shit even sounded stupid to her. The first time she got out of the house on her own, she put herself in major danger of getting knocked. She told Sticks where she was and simply said, "I'll fill you in when you get here."

Sticks said he would be there in twenty minutes. His tow truck bent the corner in fifteen minutes flat.

Lolah walked out of the sandwich shop where she had been waiting, two cop cars had already drove by the B'mer, but neither of them had stopped.

"I'm sorry for the inconvenience," she said when she got into the truck with Sticks. "You probably think I'm a real pain in the ass, huh?"

"You funny, baby girl. We all need a little help every now and again. But let me guess," he said. "This has something to do with that loud-ass butterfly you met at the mall?"

"How did you know?"

"Besides the fact that fool had trouble painted across the

back of his Tinker Bell-looking ass in neon colors? That was a pretty easy read," Sticks said. "You two went out together: You are here, and he's not."

"Pretty good, Sherlock," she had to admit.

"Whatever."

Then Lolah filled him in on what had gone down. "I didn't want to take any chances by driving the car."

"No doubt. You did the right thing," he assured her.

"I will make a phone call and dump the car and that'll be the end of it," he said in a close and shut kind of way.

Sticks acted like it was no big deal.

"Won't your father be pissed about the ride?" She knew Sticks and Matteo weren't hurting for any money, but there was no way that Sticks could get fair market value for a new BMW at the drop of a dime. "He's going to take a loss, and I will pay for it if I have to."

Sticks laughed at her naivety.

"What's so funny?" Lolah asked.

"You still have a lot to learn," he said, shaking his head.

Lolah didn't appreciate the fact that he was talking to her as if she were a child. "Fuck you." She flicked him the finger.

Sticks looked surprised that she had cursed at him, but the smile that had been glued on his face was gone.

"I wasn't laughing at you, baby girl. Don't be so hot tempered."

"Then what were you laughing at?"

"The car, I thought you knew it was a bootleg."

Lolah was too done. She frowned her face up with a mixture of confusion and surprise written all over it. "Chinese are bootlegging B'mers too. Them ma'fuckers got their hands in everything."

The beginning of a smiled formed, but Sticks quickly got rid of it. He was a quick learner.

"My bad, baby girl, for not being clear. When I say bootleg—that means that the whip is hot, the VIN number has been changed, matching a fake new title and registration, that's official, Motor Vehicles doesn't even have a way to detect it. Ya feel me?"

"Okay, I got it," she said, but was still processing the scenario of the hustle through her head.

Sticks added, "But make no mistake, the Chinese are some bad mofos too."

It took less than thirty minutes for Sticks to complete the transaction to off the BMW, and in a strange way Lolah was impressed.

They were on their way back to the house when she asked, "Is bootleg vehicles another entity of your and Matteo's business?"

"Not really. Don't have the time and energy it takes to do it right. So that everything can smooth over, between the supplier of the cars, clientele to dump them in a timely manner, babysit the folks who doctor the titles and registrations. Too time consuming, detail orientated for me. Got better shit to do with my time."

Just as Sticks completed his sentence, Lolah got an idea. Getting into the car game would be perfect for her. She knew a little about cars and had the patience to see each car through.

She also needed the money because her stash was running low and a new hustle could keep her busy as well as paid.

"I just had a thought; hear me out."

"I'm afraid to ask."

"Why don't you give me the game? Let me do it." He was quiet and was about to shut her down, but she started talking a mile a minute. "I can't live off you and your father for the rest of my life. He always tells me I'm a part of the family and he wants me to feel like it. Then I should be able to contribute to the family business. Make my own money, which I've always done. And since playing poker, doing hair or makeup is totally out, why not bootleg cars?"

When Sticks didn't answer right away, she gave him a small sample of her résumé. "I'm smart, savvy, and business minded." Then she went on to tell him about her salon and a few other ventures, legal and illegal, she had been a part of.

Sticks reluctantly shared the pros and cons of the endeavor at hand. "Trust me, it's not as easy as it sounds. Besides, if you are as good as you think you are, the competition won't like you and that could pose as a problem."

Lolah asked, "Are you afraid of the competition?" She knew the question would punch at his ego.

Sticks quickly pointed out, "It's not about being afraid or not afraid. It's about avoiding unnecessary trouble whenever possible. Ya feel me?"

"I feel ya, Sticks."

"Good."

"But also know that some waters just have to be addressed once you get to the bridge."

Sticks couldn't deny the girl could sell water to a whale, he thought, and then asked her, "Are you always this persistent when you want something?"

"Always," she said confidently.

Sticks thought for a moment before relenting. "I know this guy," he said, "that may be able to help you out with inventory, and has a few clients who would be ready to deal as quick as you get your hands on the cars."

"When can I meet him?" she asked, of the guy who could supply her with product.

"Slow down, baby girl." He made a left into their neighborhood. "He hangs out at this real fly ass club on Sunday nights. We can go and I will introduce you. You are going to have to dress to impress."

"That's who Lolah Escarda is, a glamorous chick who is definitely about that life," she reminded him.

"But no promises."

Lolah smiled. She knew that all she needed was the ropes and the introduction and she could take it from there. "I couldn't ask for anything more."

9

Expensive Grapes

"Lolah," Sticks called out from the bottom of the steps. "Man, bring your ass on if you trying to make this move."

"Here I come," she said as she applied her lipstick, then took one last glance over in the mirror.

She had been up in her quarters for the past few hours trying to pull herself together. Her father told her it was better to always be safe than sorry. To play it safe, Lolah made some changes to her appearance just in case anyone had gotten a good enough look to identify her the day before as she made her fast getaway courtesy of Lyle. She dyed her hair from jet black to a honey blond, which with her light complexion made her look more exotic and complemented the gray contacts she inserted. This transformation definitely was her best yet, totally upgrading and polishing her look to a whole other level.

The red-bottom shoes were talking, loud, saying I'm a

badass bitch, and the way she was wearing the red short dress proved it. Though Sticks was the one who had shelled out the cash for it, there was no doubt that she owned that baby. The confidence came from Sticks when she locked eyes with him. He didn't have to say it, but the look on Sticks's face when she came downstairs co-signed that she was about to knock the city of Miami dead.

Club Liv was the trendiest club on the East Coast, housed inside the famous Fontainebleau Hotel. On Sunday nights, even the biggest of the ballers needed reservations to get in. Valet parking looked like it could've been a set for the ultimate Cash Money Records video. Only MEGA ballers popped up unannounced, flashes from the paparazzi's cameras reflecting off their heads as they tried to sneak in unnoticed, which was damn near impossible.

Lolah had done as she was told, dressed to impress. The red dress was made with a low neck and no back. The material hugged her body like a convict serving life held his wife during the conjugal visits. And her shoes were killing it. The way she walked in the six-inch heels made her ass sit up like a baby in a high chair.

"Are you sure we are going to be able to get in?" Lolah asked Sticks as they were standing in the lobby with the rest of the crowd. Sticks, wearing a mocha-colored two-piece Armani with matching slip-on Ferragamo gators, complemented her ensemble like Godiva chocolate on big red strawberries.

"Don't doubt me, baby, just stand by my side," he said. "Trust me." He smiled, and said in a flirtatious way, "That's all I want from you."

"You can always count on me," she said, batting her long eyelashes. She reached for his hand and gripped it tight.

When Lolah recognized a rapper with dreads get turned away, she got worried. If he couldn't make it to the other side of Liv's doors, how would they be able to? she wondered.

Once they reached the entrance she caught a look over by the bouncer. His back was wide enough to park a small car on it. "How's it hanging, Sticks?" Right away, the oversized bouncer embraced Sticks with a brotherly handshake.

Sticks answered, "That's between me and your girlfriend." He looked to be serious as a heart attack; then he let out a small smirk. "You know how I do."

Unfazed by the shot, the bouncer said, "That's why I don't put rings on their fingers, 'cause of players like you." He patted Sticks on the back, and just like that they were inside.

A hostess who Sticks addressed as Claudette asked him if she wanted her to lead them to the good spot. She flirted with him as if Lolah wasn't standing there. She had no idea why this girl was getting under her skin. Sticks wasn't her man *yet*, but if Sticks had been Lolah's boyfriend, she may have checked the chick with a bitch-these-Louis-bout-to-be-up-your-ass look. But because their relationship was completely platonic, she let it fly.

"If you don't mind, honey." Sticks smiled like he and Claudette were close friends. "You can show me where Carlos is seated."

Claudette gave Lolah a quick, appraising glance before addressing Sticks. "Carlos is expecting you?"

He nodded, then said, "He will be, when I see him."

Claudette led the way with her ass swaying provocatively to the beat to a 2 Chainz cut, "All I want for my birthday is a big booty girl," to Carlos's table. Lolah couldn't believe how big the girl's butt was; she sucked it up that it must have had to be a product of butt shots. Carlos sat at a table near the rear of the club. He was sitting alone texting on his iPhone, with a bucket of champagne on his table.

He happened to look up and noticed them. "Sticks." The man they had come to see stood up and acknowledged them. "Long time no see." He gave him a brotherly hug. "Man, where you been?" It was apparent that he was happy to see Sticks.

"Here, there, all around."

Carlos's eyes quickly settled on Lolah. "Who is your friend?" he asked right away, looking her up and down.

Carlos was extremely handsome, Lolah thought. He had a full head of thick curly black hair, straight white teeth, and a slight Spanish accent. He was dressed to the nines, jewelry was big with lots of shiny diamonds.

"My name is Lolah," she said, holding out her hand.

Sticks was surprised when Carlos took her hand, turned it over, and kissed the back. "Indeed, the pleasure is all mine." Then he looked at his phone; there was a call coming in. He sent it to voice mail and asked Sticks to have a seat. "Maybe you can enlighten me on how many tickets one has to scratch to hit the lottery of this magnitude."

Sticks blushed.

Carlos's eyes flashed back to Lolah, lingered a second before turning to Sticks. "Clearly you are the lucky winner of the big prize."

Sticks joked, "If I had all your bread, I'd burn all mine."

At least Lolah thought he was joking anyway.

When they set down in the booth with Carlos, Claudette appeared with two additional glasses, then disappeared again, but without shooting Sticks another one of her come-fuck-me smiles.

Bitch!

Sticks told Carlos that he and Lolah were only good friends, "like family." He said, "But by no means does that mean she's available to you. I didn't bring her here as a gift to you. I brought her for business reasons, playboy."

"Business?" He seemed so confused. Then he looked at his phone and sent it to voice mail again and the same number continued to call back-to-back and he didn't bother to answer.

Sticks continued, "That's right," he said, "she wants to go into business and I told her you'd be a good ally." Lolah watched Carlos closely, the same way she did her opponent when playing cards, just like her father had taught her, looking for tales of deception. Carlos's eyes bounced from hers to Sticks, from Sticks to hers, then back to Sticks.

"You pulling my leg, right?" Carlos seemed amused at the notion of going into business with a woman. "Why would a pretty girl like her want to get in such a dirty business?"

The bastard may have been cute, Lolah thought, but he was also a chauvinist.

Sticks explained, "I haven't even told you which business she's interested in."

Carlos squinted his face as if he were in physical pain. "But all business is ugly, especially the ones I deal in." He added, "Definitely no place for a woman."

Lolah pulled out all of her chips and placed them in the pot. She spoke up for herself, "It's simple." She crossed her legs. "I want to bootleg cars. I don't need a babysitter or your money as any kind of investments. I have my own money, and plenty of it. So, I don't need no handouts. But . . ." she paused for a second and let her eyes meet Carlos's. "I do want your services. If I can get them, I'll be grateful. In return, I'll give you my loyalty, and I assure you my loyalty is something that can't be wavered or brought. I promise at the end of the day to make you enough money for you to appreciate and respect me." Placing her hands on the side on his thigh, she said, "You feel me?"

Through his pants, Carlos's body temperature rose, and Lolah was sure it wasn't the only thing on his body that was going up.

"Maybe we can do some business," Carlos said, "but"— he put his finger up—"on a trial basis. Give me a day or so to stew over the . . . uh . . . proposition, and I'll get back to you. Is this to your satisfaction?"

Sticks couldn't believe what had just transgressed. No one ever demanded anything from Carlos, especially not a woman and a woman he had never seen or knew nothing about. Lolah smiled seductively knowing that he'd see things her way.

"I couldn't ask for anything more."

"Let's all have a drink—enough of this business talk, *si?*"

Carlos filled their glasses and proposed a toast. "To friends over business."

They all touched glasses and took a sip of twelve-hundred-dollar-a-bottle expensive grapes.

10

Nobody Likes a Greedy Bitch

In a matter of days, Sticks turned Lolah on to major buyers of stolen cars, one in Russia and the other in Argentina. Dealing with Lolah was like Burger King: a buyer could have it any way they wanted—make, model, interior color, features, and everything. If her clients wanted it, she got her guys to go get it for her. Everything was working out; the supply and demand were leveling out.

Though things were pretty much intact, she wanted to figure out a way that she could eliminate the middleman on the shipping end. The only problem was the logistics, out of the country. But the beauty of any business was one step at a time, she reminded herself. She was already getting well ahead of herself, before venturing into large overseas markets; she first needed to get her money up in the States. So she started with shipping cars over to the Bahamas, but she couldn't resist the Russian's money because it was always long and right.

She had only been in business a little over two months,

and her profit alone was already tripling the paper she left Richmond with. She was off to a better than decent start and able to rent out an office space near the beach. She could tell that Sticks was impressed with her negotiating skills and business acumen. In addition, she felt like she was in her element. It was something about making that money and keeping busy that made her think less about home, especially since she had touched base with her father and he was okay. But most of all, he was most proud that she was surviving, eating good, and enjoying her life in the land of the free.

In Mickey's eyes, that was all any father could really ask for. He knew he'd made the right decision in sending her to Florida. Matteo and Sticks owed him—harboring a fugitive was a small favor in return for the pain they'd caused all those years ago when they lived in Virginia. That's one of the reasons Mickey tried to talk to Peaches about her growing attachment to her new family.

"I know they treating you real well, but I don't want you to get too attached," Mickey told Peaches during one of his calls.

"Why do you say that? Aren't they your friends from back in the day?" For Peaches, Mickey's caution was coming a bit too late. She had already caught feelings for Sticks and knew he felt the same way. They hadn't burned up the sheets yet, but it was only a matter of time.

All Mickey would say was, "We got history that's both good and bad. I don't want you getting hurt."

But not everyone wanted Peaches to be happy. That was evident by the text message left on her phone just this morning:

**NOBODY LIKES A GREEDY BITCH EATING RIGHT OFF THEIR PLATE.
BE CAREFUL NOT TO CHOKE!**

Lolah wasn't intimidated, but she wasn't stupid either. With her vision and ambition, she knew that she'd be stepping on someone's toes. After all, both Sticks and Carlos had warned her about this from the beginning. She had no idea that he would take notice of her this early in the game! Also, she was thoroughly impressed that he was able to get her number and contact her.

From day one, she researched her competition in depth. There were lots of car thieves, a few small timers, who stole cars, chopped them, and sold the parts. But the only big-time player buying and selling high-end cars in volume was Pablo. Pablo had a reputation for being an asshole with a serious mean streak. From the information Lolah gathered, he seemed to have more bark than bite, but that didn't mean Pablo wasn't to be taken seriously. She had learned at a young age, never sleep on an enemy and especially never underestimate their capabilities.

Lolah had a crazy morning already. Everything that could go wrong was going wrong, and to top it all off, she had a bad case of cramps and wasn't really in the mood for the excuses, no's, or any bullshit, but if she were a toilet, she was stopped up from the shit going on in her business.

She sat at the desk, with her legs crossed and the phone on speaker. "What do you mean the cars are gone?"

"Nothing personal, Lolah. But I got a better offer for the Vette," Dean said.

"What about the six Benzs you said you would get for

me?" she asked him, knowing in her gut that he didn't have those either, but she so wanted to be wrong.

"They gone too," Dean said.

"They gone too?" she asked, not expecting or allowing him to answer. "Really?" She shook her head as if he could see her through the phone.

He and Lolah had made a deal for twenty cars a week at 7k each. Dean and his crew were beasts at circumventing alarms and snatching whips, but obviously not very keen on loyalty. "Maybe next time I will do better," Dean suggested.

Dean had been the second supplier today that had reneged on a deal; it was crystal clear what was going on. Pablo had paid a better price for them not to sell to her. But what Pablo didn't know was she was a master at cards, and he wasn't the only one who could deal from the bottom. First she would deal with Dean since he was on her radar right then. "I tell you what I'm going to do," she said confidently, as if she was in a position to make him an offer he couldn't refuse. "I'm going to put Pablo's ass out of business, for starters"—she took a sip of her cappuccino and then started speaking firmly again—"and when you come begging for someone to sell your merchandise to, I'm going to tell you to drive them up your fat ass. Mark my words."

"Why you acting like that, Lolah? It's only business, like I said. It's nothing personal with you. In fact, I like you." He was trying to hedge his bets by playing both ends to the middle.

Lolah quoted a line that she liked from *Scarface*, "All you have in this world is your word and your balls." She added:

"I suggest you use plenty of spit the next time you suck on Pablo's."

She disconnected the phone call angrily. She knew she now had to step up her game.

Sticks walked in her office staring at her, smiling. "I'd hate to be on your bad side," he said. "Take it easy, Dr. Jekyll, or are you Mrs. Hyde today?"

Lolah punched him on the shoulder. "Ha. Ha, Mr. Funny Man. Let's let go eat before boobirds come out and start to try to crap on ya."

They headed to lunch and as soon as she got to the restaurant, she realized that she had left her phone in the car. She ran to the car to get the phone lying on the seat of the car. As she about to cross the street to head back inside, she was checking the call log, and she happened to look up. That's when she noticed a black SUV speeding in her direction. Her first thought was it was the police who had finally caught up with her. If she didn't know better she thought it was coming directly for her. And it was. It was a good thing she had great reflexes and darted out of the way of the fast-moving vehicle.

11

Wanted: Hard-Body Goons

Lolah was so pissed it was difficult to think straight. Not only had the driver of the SUV attempted to run her over, he caused her to ruin her new Giuseppes.

Sticks asked her to take it easy and gave her a bottle of water. "Thank you." Lolah plopped down on the plush sofa. Matteo was out taking care of something or another; she and Sticks had the house to themselves. Sticks was trying to be objective. He said, "What if it really was an accident? The man driving the truck might have been drunk or texting."

"And a reindeer may really be able to fly when nobody's looking," she shot back. "The driver of that truck tried to kill me or make me believe that he was trying to kill me. It was as simple as that."

Sticks twisted the cap off of his own bottle of water and took a sip. "And you think Pablo set it up?" Sticks questioned, "How could he know you would be at that place at that time?"

Lolah didn't believe in coincidences. "I don't think, I

know Pablo was behind it. Maybe he had someone following me and knows where the office is? That's not the most important thing concerning me."

Shaking his head, Sticks said, "You don't think it's important to know if someone has been following you?"

"I said, it's not the *most* important thing. We can't change what 'has been,' only what's to come next."

Sometimes it was hard to believe that Lolah was only twenty-one, seven years younger than him. She was as smart and cunning as she was gorgeous. A dangerous combination. "I'm almost afraid to ask," he said, wanting to see where her mind was. "But what's next?"

An almost giddy gleam shown from her eyes, but it was completely absent from the rest of her face. "Now we are getting somewhere," she said. "Tell me, how quick can you put your hands on some hard-body goons who can be trusted?"

Like Lolah, Sticks was no virgin to the streets, and had learned its ways at a young age. "You know the flava of the day. Money talks and bullshit walks. Let's be clear, though, nobody can be completely trusted. That's something earned and rare. But, yeah, I know a few guys."

Lolah nodded. "Good enough. I'm trying to buy a goon, not a husband. Complete trust isn't wholeheartedly required. Just good people who gonna ride for me."

"I know just the person then."

"And this is what I have in mind . . ."

12

A Live-Ass Coward

Pablo, the youngest of twelve siblings, escaped Cuba in the oppressive fist of Fidel Castro at the age of seventeen. He journeyed the rough Atlantic Ocean in a boat about the size of a bathtub that almost killed him at least twice. But he overcame the odds, crashing safely on the shores of Miami alive. Bruised, battered, and broke, but alive. That was twenty years ago and today Pablo had done pretty well for himself. He owned two homes and a couple of boats. Real boats. Nothing like that piece of driftwood he escaped from back in the day. These were 75- and 90-foot vessels. He also held the reins to four warehouse-style garages, where he stored and managed his inventory of stolen cars. Pablo spent most of his time in a small, yet lucrative, chop shop a few blocks away from the American Airlines arena. That's where he was this evening, in a tiny office nestled in the back of a chop shop. A continual racket from all the air tubes and hydraulic lifts filled the shop dirty. Pablo liked the noise; noise meant money was being made, and he loved dinero.

He opened the door to his office, "Miquel! Get in here. Pronto."

Miquel, a couple of years from being old enough to legally drink, was an illegal immigrant from Nicaragua. He couldn't speak English worth a damn, but the dude could strip a car down to the horn and then put it back together in his sleep.

In his native tongue, Miguel asked, *"Que pasa?"* He wore dirty blue overalls and a pair of Dickie boots that leaned to the side. Underneath his fingernails were permanently black from the accumulation from the dirt oil and grime. Miquel liked them that way; in his mind, it showed he was a hard worker.

"I got six Benzs coming through in a couple of hours." Pablo spoke fluent English but used Spanish with Miquel. "I'm going to need you to stay late tonight."

Miquel was trying to save enough money to send back home to his four brothers and two sisters. He would stay up all night if he had to. Sleep would come once he accomplished his goals. Pablo knew this and used this to his advantage, never cutting the poor guy any slack and paying him the very bare minimum.

"Ningún problema," Miquel said with a proud smile.

In a white two-piece linen suit and two-inch padded lifts in his loafers, Pablo looked out of place in the garage, as the Pope would in a whorehouse. However, he thought that white made him look important. Before coming to America, he never owned anything white. Now he wore white clothes, obsessed over his white teeth, and drove only white cars.

Pablo picked up a pack of Camels from his desk and after

shaking two from the pack, he handed one to Miquel and placed the other into the corner of his brown lips. Miquel hated the taste of cigarettes, especially the harsh-tasting Camels that Pablo smoked, but he never told Pablo that.

"*Gracias,*" Miquel said before lighting up.

And that's when all hell broke loose.

Gunshots rang out from automatic weapons. It sounded like microwave popcorn being popped through a megaphone. Bullets sparked holes through bodies of cars, ricocheting off the grease-stained concrete floors.

Miquel was reaching in his pocket for something when a 40 cal ripped through the chest of his overalls. The bullet exited from his back, leaving a hole the size of a fist. Miquel lay there bleeding with his Camel clinched between his teeth looking to Pablo for help, but Pablo was only worried about himself.

Pablo threw his hands in the air. "No weapon! I don't have a weapon! Please don't shoot."

Pablo thanked Santa Maria when the shooting stopped. He then kissed his fingers, making the sign of the cross over his chest.

Five men had raided the chop shop in all. They were paid not to kill, but teach Pablo some manners. However, if someone happened to have gotten in the way of a bullet or tried to be a hero, that was their own fault.

T-Rex was 6'6" and built like a tank, working out every day for over ten years while doing time for robbery. T-Rex asked, "Are you Pablo?" while the other four hired guns held the shop down.

The other four men had no need for words because a smoking gun was multilingual. No one who wasn't already dead wanted to join the unlucky.

T-Rex said, "I'm not going to ask but one mo' time. I'm talking to you, Tattoo." T-Rex raised the Uzi he held for emphasis. "Are you Pablo or not?"

Pablo's mouth was as dry as a field of cotton during a heat wave; he barely choked out the words, "Yes, I . . . I am Pablo." He knew that he was hopeless without his muscle and pissed that he had let them go home early.

"Good," said T-Rex, speaking around the toothpick in his mouth. "I came to do you a favor."

Pablo thought he was going to be sick. A gas bubble burst in his stomach. He farted, almost shitting his drawers. In a shaky voice, he asked, "What type of favor?"

With a straight face, T-Rex said, "The best kind. The type that if you do what the fuck you are told, maybe you will live long enough to thank me one day."

Pablo asked, "What would I owe . . . the favor you offered me?"

"I'm pretty easy to get along with, Tattoo. All that's required is that you discontinue all business in the state of Florida. That's all."

A wise man once told Pablo, "If you quit while you are ahead, it's not considered quitting." Back then, Pablo didn't understand the meaning of those words, but today the meaning was loud and clear. An alive coward beats a dead tuff guy any day.

Pablo said, "I'm willing to agree to those conditions."

13

Be Careful What You Ask

"That was the best twenty thou I ever spent," Lolah said, referring to the money that she had paid to T-Rex and his boys.

"Thanks."

Sticks had not only located the muscle to do the job, he totally surprised Lolah by offering to pay half the cost to do the service.

"That's what friends do for one another," he said.

They sat in the kitchen nook, which was backdropped by a giant bay window, eating breakfast. The view of the orange and lemon trees growing in the backyard was amazing. Sticks had cooked breakfast for the two of them. Cheese eggs with bacon, home-style potatoes, and biscuits.

Lolah asked Sticks to pass the jelly. There was a magnetic energy when their hands touched over the jar. More and more, Lolah had been feeling a certain type of way around him. He was handsome, generous, and thoughtful—qualities that were hard for a girl to ignore. As she spread the strawberry preserves on one of the biscuits, Lolah thanked him again.

Sticks's mouth was full of food, when he asked, "What are you thanking me for now?" Then he swallowed his eggs and smiled. "Not that it matters much. I enjoy the attention of a beautiful and smart girl anytime I can get it."

Now it was Lolah's turn to smile. "So you think I'm beautiful, huh?"

Lolah watched Sticks blush. Over the last few months, Sticks had turned up the heat between them, acting more like her man than a protective big brother.

"Girl, you look in the mirror every damn day, at least five times or another, so if you don't know you have it going on by now, your ass must be either blind or crazy." Sticks's gaze caressed her body before returning to her face. He was definitely feeling her.

Lolah enjoyed watching him pretend to beat around the bush. "That wasn't what I asked," she teased. "The question was, what did you think?"

"I think you are fucking with me, that's what. And you best be careful, you might get what you looking for." But even as he dared her, he wondered what she would think of him if she knew he was responsible for her mother's death.

14

And Their Eyes Were
Watching

Lolah was running late but looking still stunning, like she'd just walked out of the pages of a cover of a fashion magazine as she made her way to the Prime One Twelve Restaurant. On those days, when the Miami heat wasn't taking prisoners, she liked to go home, freshen up, and change when the sun went down. Today she didn't have the time to make it home due to the timing of the phone call she received from Carlos saying that it was important that they met. Since she was not only famished and minutes away, she made her way to South Beach to talk business over dinner with him.

Carlos greeted her in front of the Prime One Twelve Restaurant with a friendly hug and kiss on the cheek. She tried to read his body language for a tell as to why it was so urgent that they meet. Either she was getting rusty or there wasn't anything wrong, because Carlos looked super relaxed and jovial.

Not knowing why else he would invite her to a sit-down, she couldn't resist jumping straight to the matter at hand. She leaned in closer to him and spoke in a tone a little above a whisper. "Is everything okay with the shipment?" She held her breath awaiting an answer. Most of her profit had gone into the upcoming shipment.

"For sure," he assured her by way of locking eyes with her. "Everything is running smooth. Your order had already been filled, all except two cars. But no worries, my guys should be acquiring these last two now as we speak. Everything will be straight by sunrise." Carlos spoke with a chest inflated with confidence that could have easily been mistaken for arrogance "But, you know, I never disappoint."

If Lolah had to predict the future dealings with Carlos based on his past ones, she would have to concur. "Truly you don't, and I appreciate that."

From the day after the night Sticks had introduced them at the club, Carlos had been coming through with the cars he promised on a weekly basis. Like clockwork, he always delivered exactly what she asked for down to the last detail or better. And in return, she always had his money, and it was never short or late, and depending on her mood, she usually dropped a tip, or incentive, to show him her appreciation for doing good business. Over the two months she had been pushing her business full-fledge, Carlos wasn't the only person whom she brought merchandise from, but he'd turned into her go-to provider. Dependability was an underrated characteristic.

Unlike Dean, Carlos treated his word as his bond and he lived by it. Carlos was very passionate and extremely precise about his business. However, that didn't stop him from constantly flirting with Lolah. She didn't appreciate it but could handle it. There was no denying his passion and dedication to getting the job done. The guys on his team could pluck anything from Jettas to Jaguars, but they specialized in getting Lambos, Bentleys, Rolls, and anything else exotic she desired. Lolah still wasn't sure how they procured their inventory with the keys always enclosed. Even sometimes going straight to the dealerships and rolling them off the showroom floors, making her being able to offer her clients any and all German engineering. She was grateful to have Carlos on her team, but more blessed that he was as loyal as he was.

If the shipment was point as scheduled, then why the impromptu meeting? she wondered. With Pablo now running for the border and out of the picture, she couldn't possibly think of any other issues it could be. Maybe Carlos wanted more money, she thought. She had made a sweetheart deal with him and was upping his status on the playing field in a major way in the short time they'd been working together. Besides, she didn't take Carlos to be a greedy kind of dude. However, money changed some people in a major way. Some folks get it and they turn into monsters, wanting more and more of it, making them almost impossible to deal with. Whatever the situation was, Lolah surmised, she'd deal with it accordingly. She didn't push any further; there would be plenty of time to get to the bottom of it once they were seated.

"Nice place! Fancy," she said as she strutted inside the restaurant. Although she'd heard about it and Sticks had been promising to bring her there, this was her first time there and she was totally impressed with the place he selected for them to dine. The restaurant was definitely a trendy and expensive place to be seen amongst the Who's Who of Miami.

Once they were seated and all the different servers had finally done their spills and filled their glasses with water, "We'll have a bottle of Ace of Spades," Carlos said with confidence.

"Really. Big spender, huh?" She poured on her charm. "What's the high spirits and celebrating all about?" she asked with enthusiasm. Carlos was filled with so much excitement it was almost contagious.

"Just everything," he said with a big grin showing more than half his pearly whites.

Lolah hated when people spoke in such broad terms. She was the type who liked details and people to be specific, but she rolled with the punches, "Aww, like?" Lolah probed after taking a sip of her water.

Carlos's eyes sparked with an inner glow. "Like you?" His eyes beamed. "Like this money we making. Like how quick this shit rolling in."

The discussion of money and success always got Lolah energized and revved up. "I will damn sure toast to that." The mood had definitely lightened. "In fact, they need to hurry up and bring us that bottle then."

Normally she wasn't a big drinker, an occasional sip or two here and there, but tonight was a different. She knew that truly this buzz belonged to her and she had a lot to be grateful for. She reflected on the conditions that had brought her to Miami and where she was now. She had definitely taken her busted hand and turned it into a straight flush.

While waiting for the champagne to arrive, Lolah and Carlos reminisced about their first meeting.

"Who'd have thought we'd end up here. Right?"

Not in a million years, Lolah thought, but kept it to herself. "I'm sure you thought Sticks was delusional and I was crazy," she said.

He nodded a little. "Crazy sexy," he added. "But I knew that you were real, because Sticks is so official. And I'm glad that I rolled the dice on you, though," he said.

"Me too," she said with a smile. "But, Carlos, we still have so much more to accomplish." She took his hand and leaned into his ear. "There is so much more money to be made, you know."

"Yes, I believe in you, your cause, and your movement. I'm going to continue to follow your lead," he said. And that's when the bottle arrived at the table.

The waiter filled their glasses and Carlos told her, "Raise your glass, beautiful." She did what she was told. "Here's to you. A woman who knows exactly what she wants and has no qualms about doing whatever it takes to get it. To money, power, respect, good health, and never needing any get-out-of-jail-free cards. But most of all, to our bond of loyalty that we continue to forge. I guess to sum it up: great friends, lots of business, and cash by the millions. Here's to you, Ms. Lolah Escarda!"

"Aww," she said, tickled by how genuine Carlos seemed. Lolah said, "I'll drink to that." And she did. Despite the bubbles, champagne went down so easy that there was no need for babysitting the rest of it. A moment later, her glass was damn near empty. The waiter earning the huge tip he would get when the night was over didn't miss a beat refilling their glasses.

Right after dinner came and they had finished their meals, Carlos reached in his pocket and produced a small blue box, catching her totally by surprise. "For you, my lady."

The gift caught her totally off guard. "Oh, no, I can't," she said, leaving him holding it in his hand.

If her hesitance to accept the box had offended him, Carlos didn't show it. "It's nothing serious, just a small token of my appreciation. Please open it," he insisted with wide puppy dog eyes.

It was a mixture between the champagne and Carlos' persistence that induced her into letting her guard down, accepting and opening the box. Inside was a diamond necklace with a small pendant of a car, which resembled a vintage Bentley. The tires were black diamonds and the steering wheel was blue topaz. The body of the car was iced out in white diamonds, so clear and big that they bounced off the lights in the restaurant. "Oh my goodness, Carlos, how gorgeous." She was almost speechless while examining the piece. "Seriously, you really shouldn't have!" It was beautiful, but it was also too much. She didn't want to blur the lines.

"You deserve it. It's for good luck. And the blue topaz

will protect you from all that attempts to harm or hurt you." The passionate glint in his eyes was sincere. "Trust me, it will protect you in the midst of all the evil or enemy that tries to attack you. I took the piece myself to be blessed, so stop overanalyzing the fact that it came from me, and put the thing on and accept your blessings properly."

Lolah thought about what Carlos had said, and she wasn't superstitious. She believed that people created their own luck. In her eyes, there were no magic gifts and curses, but she kept those beliefs to herself and allowed him to place the necklace around her neck.

"Thank you, Carlos. I appreciate you." She got up and kissed him on the cheek. "I really do." She sat down. "No words could ever express my gratitude on how you've never wavered when it came to me, especially with all the Pablo drama. You didn't know me from Adam and you trusted me, and you stayed down for me."

He interrupted her, "Well, Sticks is good peoples and he wouldn't turn me on to no bullshit."

"You are right."

"I want you to know," Carlos said from the heart, "that you've been as much of a gift to me as you may think I've been to you. I also want you to know that I worry about you sometimes. Hell—I worry about you a lot."

Lolah was touched by his empathy, but she didn't need it.

"Trust and believe," she assured him, "I can take care of myself. You have no idea. Been doing it for a minute."

Not ready to let the subject lie, Carlos said, "I know you're a tough cookie, but this here Miami animal is a different beast that's inundated with fuck boys."

Lolah wasn't sure if she wanted to hear the answer, but she had to ask the question.

"What do you mean by fuck boys?" She hoped this wasn't his way of saying he was bisexual. He didn't look the type that would take it up the ass, but she'd seen stranger shit in the past.

"Fuck boys—that's my name for chumps who have big-money dreams and piggy bank hustles. So they prey on the next man's hustle, or woman in your case. Gender don't really matter to a fuck boy. He try his hand wherever he thinks he can get away with it."

"I won't spend a lot of time worrying about fuck boys, but I will, as always, proceed with caution."

"You've made more money in two months than a lot of wannabes see in a lifetime," he told her. "Just be careful. That type of bread breed crabs by the bushels."

His words were hitting too close to home, and the champagne was making it more intense. She knew she was tipsy and not one hundred percent in control—and that was means for a slipup that could cost her everything. And that was a problem. It was time for her to go and get to her safe haven that she had created at Matteo's house.

Although the evening had turned out better than she anticipated, Lolah declined dessert. As Carlos waited on the bill to come, they continued to talk, but Carlos was staring at her in a way that he was undressing her with his eyes. "You are so gorgeous, Lolah." He reminded her too many times to count and she knew what he had on his mind. But it wasn't that kind of party.

"You should definitely let me have one night with you. Show you just one time how much I appreciate you."

"No, sir, now you know we can't mix business and pleasure." Just then the waiter approached the table with the check. "Ah," she said, "saved by the bell, the bill."

"Yeah," Carlos smiled, and joked, "I'm glad I don't have to sit through that lecture, Lolah," as he put a few hundred dollar bills into the binder to pay for their tab.

"Glad I don't have to give it to you then." She smiled.

"You can't fault me for trying." They stood up. "After all, you are a stunningly gorgeous woman, with lots of charisma, spunk, style, ambition, a hell of a body and—" He put his finger up as he led them out. "And . . . rich, I must add. That's a complete package."

"You got that right," she said, blushing.

The two laughed and giggled all over the place as they waited for the valet to bring their cars around. Carlos's phone kept vibrating; it had been all night.

"You really should get that," Lolah said.

He shooed off her comment with his hand. "Aww, no time for foolishness when we are celebrating our future," he said, powering the phone completely off and putting it in his pocket.

Carlos was so into impressing Lolah and enjoying the moment with her, while Lolah was so drunk that she had totally let her guard down, for the first time since being in Miami, and wasn't checking her surroundings that neither noticed that they were being watched . . . and definitely by the wrong set of eyes.

15

The Little Things

Once in her car, she reached into her Hermes bag and checked her phone. She saw a couple of missed calls from Matteo; he was always checking on her. Since he had loosened the reins on her, she usually called him on a regular basis to keep him up on what she was doing, so he wouldn't worry himself to death.

Then there was a missed call and text from Sticks: **u ok beautiful?**

Even though Sticks's text was short and sweet, it melted her heart because she knew it was sincere and from the heart. Sticks was nothing like the other guys whom she'd encountered back home; he was everything that her father would have wanted for her.

Things were finally shaping up for her and there was no doubt about it, things happen for a reason. There was a reason why she landed in Miami and why of all the men she interacted with on regular basis, Sticks was the only one who caught her attention. Like her father always said, what is meant to be will be. And things always have a way of working out for the best.

Lolah was not only feeling herself but the liquor. Her feelings were running wild, and when the phone rang, she looked at the caller ID. It was the perfect person she felt to share her feelings with. He always gave her the best advice.

"Hello."

"How are you, princess?"

"I'm good."

"You sound drunk," Mickey said. He knew his daughter like a book. She was the love of his life. For the past fourteen years since Emma died, up until Peaches had to flee the city, she had been his whole existence. He knew that girl in and out, and the fact she was almost a thousand miles away didn't change it.

"You drunk, girl?"

"No, Daddy, not drunk, just had a little champagne. Just celebrating with one of my business associates our accomplishments, that's all," she said; then she slammed on the horn. "Lady, what are you doing?" she screamed at a Cadi that cut her off.

"And you're drinking and driving?" he asked. She could hear the disappointment in his voice.

"Noooo, it's not like that," she tried to assure her father, who was quiet for a moment trying to assess the situation.

"So you are not driving?" he asked.

"I'm about to pull over and I'm going to sit in this gas station parking lot and talk to my favorite guy right now."

"Right now?" he questioned. "I thought I was your favorite guy, you mean to tell me somebody is taking my place?" Mickey lightened the mood with a joke. Though he wasn't happy, he didn't want to spend the limited minutes he did have fussing with his daughter.

"No, nobody could ever take your place, Daddy. In fact, I've been having this whole topic on my mind for a couple of weeks now and wanted to get your input on it."

"Shoot, baby," he said, loving that although his daughter was a long ways away from home, she still wanted to share her feelings and issues with him. That made him feel good on the inside.

"Well, I'm making quite a good life for myself here, one that you would be proud of. If I have to say so myself, Daddy, I really did well with picking up the pieces."

"I heard," he said, letting her know in no uncertain way that he'd been talking to Matteo, checking up on her.

"One that you'd be proud of. Everything you taught me"—she took a deep breath—"it really prepared me for the sharks, wolves, snakes, and the whales, too, and they are learning slowly but surely that they don't want to mess with me. That I swim in deep waters, Daddy."

"Then I did something right." She could hear the smile that she had just put on her father's face.

"You did a wonderful job, you did that." She complimented her father and she could feel his heart soften through the phone. She could feel the warmth in his voice. "And I know you know this, but you really prepared me for this journey, but there was one thing that either I cut class or you didn't prep for."

"What's that?" Mickey was curious and had no clue what

she could possibly be referring to. Because the girl was literally raised in the streets, she'd seen a lot more than any twenty-one-year-old he knew.

"Just my feelings."

"Feelings?" He was puzzled.

"You taught me to never let my emotions override my intellect. My body is a temple, and that whoever I'm with, I should know that I'm the prize, never to be a pawn." She rambled on some of the jewels of love her father had given her. "Like who likes me, and who loves less controls the relationship. Keep my mind on my money. No man is worth me putting my dreams and aspirations to the side. Yes, you taught me those things."

"Yes, I did, and, darling, those are very key things."

"Yes, they are, Daddy. They are."

"Then what seems to be the problem, pumpkin?" he asked.

"Before all this happened, you always told me, you never wear my heart on my sleeve. And to never fall in love, just to grow in love. And I never fully understood that. But I took your advice, and after a while of dealing with the same knucklehead I realized I didn't want to grow it. But now it's different and extra complicated.

"I'm in this situation, which I know at any given time I have to be able to walk away from at a moment's notice. However, I'm around this person who I've grown into strong like and they like me too. A guy who takes care of me but cares for me, who respects me, who is honest, watches my back, makes me laugh, laughs at my jokes, understands me as much as I will let him, accepts me for who I am, flaws and all."

"That's what a man should do," Mickey said firmly.

"And I really like him too. I mean, I feel like I don't have any control of my heart when I am around him. Sometimes when he walks in the room, and when I hear his ringtone, I can't hide my smile. And you know I can read people, everything about him from the first day I met him has been genuine. Even when I get out of control, he tells me about myself. But you know what the really crazy part is, Daddy?"

"What?"

"That when he tells me I'm talking crazy or doing something out of pocket, I respect that and I know he cares and it is coming from a real place."

Mickey had to agree. "He must be someone special if you actually care about his opinion. I know firsthand that you are stubborn as a bull." Mickey was about to say more, but she cut him off.

"Daddy, I really like this guy, but it's just complicated with my current overall predicament."

"I understand," he said, thinking about her situation, but wanting and needing to know more for his own reasons and to give her the best possible guidance under the circumstances. "Where do you two stand now?" he asked.

Before she could answer, the phone beeped again; less than ten percent of the battery was left. "Well, it's just intense emotions running wild. Nothing has happened sexually, but we both have a magnetic attraction to each other. He hasn't made any advances and has been totally respectable. We've been friends and just spend a lot of time going out and hanging out as solely friends, which is getting a little awkward because we mesh so well. And I know that we both want more, but we haven't taken it to the next level."

"Who is this person and has Matteo met him? And what does he say?"

She paused for a second. "It's his son."

Lolah's phone went dead, but not before Mickey blurted out, "You have got to be fucking kidding me."

16

Combat Princess

Lolah sat in the car in the parking lot of the U-gas station wiggling the iPhone charger around, trying to get it to work for her. She had been in the middle of the conversation with her father and wanted to hear what he had to say. She knew that the charger had a short in it and had been meaning to pick up a new one. "Damn it," she said. "I've got to do better," she scolded herself. Then finally the green light popped back on. She had it working, but she knew that her father probably wouldn't be calling her back. Would she have to wait two weeks for him to call again? Her feelings were running rapid. And she knew that she needed to get home, get her feelings under control and herself under the covers to sleep the alcohol off.

She started the car, and all of a sudden, "BOOM!"

"You've got to be fucking kidding me."

A Range Rover had hit her parked beautiful convertible Bentley at full speed, moving it inches from the door of the station. The hit was so hard that it tossed the few contents out of the car, her purse and a couple of CD cases, onto the pavement. At first she didn't know what was going on. She looked in her side-view mirror and saw the door of the Rover opening and someone getting out. At first she was sure that the person was going to bring her their insurance information.

"Bitch." She heard a woman's voice.

"What the hell?" she said out loud as if someone could hear her. She knew that these Miami people were crazy, and this woman had the nerve to hit her car and then want to talk shit. This night was getting more interesting by the minute.

"Bittttttttttttttccccccccccchhhhhh!" the woman screamed again.

Now this woman had to be either drunk, high, or fucking deranged, Peaches thought. But Peaches wasn't taking no chances. At that moment she wished she had a pistol, but she didn't. So to be on the safe side, she ran her hand down along the side of the seat and grabbed the billy club that she had gotten from Matteo, who had gotten it from a police friend of his.

"Bitttttttttttccccchhhhhhh," the woman was screaming at the top of her lungs, prompting Peaches to reach into the glove box and get her Mace.

Her first thought was that maybe it was Pablo, and he was coming to retaliate. But then she heard a high-pitched woman's voice with a Latin accent, screaming, "Bitch, get out the car," which made her think again. She'd always imagined Pablo would have sent men dressed in black for her, who moved in silence and violence.

She knew there were a lot of certified cuckoo birds in Miami, but she wasn't expecting them to come mess with her. After all, Lolah kept a low profile for the most part, and didn't bother a soul. She was a free spirit and didn't want any problems. Lolah wasn't really a fighter, but she grew up in the hood, and had had her share of days of scrapping in the middle of the street. And she knew it was either be a predator or prey; and she wasn't about to be anybody's dinner in this dog-eat-dog world.

"Bitch, get the fuck out of the car," the woman screamed again.

Lolah looked in her side-view mirror and saw a pretty Spanish-looking girl dressed in camouflaged combat pants, a top to match, with some tan Timberland boots. The one thing that she couldn't miss, more than anything, and this picture will always be plastered in her head, was the girl looked like she had a whole bottle of baby oil on her face. Lolah knew what time it was.

The Vaseline on this girl's face made it clear that she came to fight and there were no ifs, ands, or buts about it. Lolah normally tried to walk away from fights, but there was no getting out of this run-in. It was what it was.

"Bitch, I'm going to teach you a lesson about fucking with me and mine." The girl spoke in English with a strong Spanish accent and was almost near the car.

Lolah quickly slipped out her Giuseppes and slipped on her flats that she always kept in the floor of her car for driving and pushed the door open.

"Get the fuck outta here, you simple-acting, loud-ass bitch. 'Cause you really don't know me."

"No, bitch, you don't know me." Combat Princess hit the back of the Bentley, then displayed her switchblade. "I'm going to fuck that pretty face of yours up, so no man will ever want your ass again."

"Aww, you got weapons, huh?" Lolah asked with a chuckle.

"To teach your ass a lesson."

"That's impossible, boo-boo," Lolah said, sizing up this girl. "They wouldn't give you a degree to teach underwater basket weaving."

"When I'm done with you, you won't be getting no more presents from no man."

"I'm self-made," Lolah said with great pride, holding her billy club ready to take this broad's head off, but at that moment realizing that this had nothing to do with her but everything to do with Carlos.

"Bitch, you done. In this town you are done."

"Bitch, you talk too much. And empty promises, I don't need 'em. Get the fuck outta here before you get hurt." Lolah tried to warn the girl.

When Combat Princess saw the billy club, she picked up a rock and threw it at Lolah.

"Seriously . . ." Lolah ducked and went to Combat Princess's ass. She was aiming to cluck her upside the head and knock some sense into it, but Combat Princess put her arm up and her forearm got caught instead. Then Lolah pushed her down on the ground and put her foot on her throat, taking the wind out of her.

"Now, I don't know what this is about, bitch, and I don't

know you and you don't know me. Now, listen, Carlos and I are in business, that's it that's all. End of story."

With all her might she got up the strength to say, "You lie."

"Now out of respect for him, I'm not going to fuck you up. Now take your ass home and go fuck Carlos so you don't have to worry about any women. And frankly, you are too cute for this stupid shit." She reached down and pinched her on the cheek.

Combat Princess wanted to say something, but she couldn't get enough strength up.

That's when Lolah heard sirens, which alerted her that she was in danger and that she needed to get her ass up and out of there before she be dealing with way bigger problems.

She ran to the car, and on her way, she grabbed her purse off the cement. Combat Princess got up as quick as she could, too, and started to make her way to the Range, but not before screaming out, "This ain't over, bitch. And stay the fuck away from Carlos. Next time I'll kill you."

Lolah couldn't believe this chick. She asked herself out loud, "What the fuck?"

She started the Bentley and tried to put up the top, but it was stuck. She pulled out of the gas station and looked in the rearview mirror to make sure that the Range was too. But she saw that Combat Princess had stopped to pick up something, and that's when Lolah realized it, "Damn, this bitch got my fucking wallet."

17

The Next Level

It is common to see quarter-million-dollar cars cruising the streets of Miami, but not with a side panel or rear end caved in. Trying to make it all the way to Matteo's house was definitely a risk not worth taking. The fact that Lolah had been drinking didn't help the situation at all. She parked the car and called Sticks. Sticks could tow the Bentley to the garage, and in a matter of a few days the car would be fixed and as good as new. She could deal with Carlos's psycho-ass wife later. The only downside to that scenario was, if there was one, that she would be further indebted to Sticks. She would have to live with that. However, she promised herself that she would one day pay him back. Somehow.

The Ritz Hotel sat on the right side of the street from where she was at. Both of them decided that a hotel would be a better place to wait than a restaurant or bar. Less scrutiny.

As Lolah pulled up, the valet attendant peeped that the car had been in a collision.

She got out and handed him the keys. "Can you park it near the back for me?" When the attendant looked at her questioningly, she added, "My jealous husband can be controlling sometimes. I'm just trying to stay off radar for a while. I may even leave him this time, who knows."

The attendant bought the story. "I will take care of everything," he said, and parked the Bentley.

Once in the lobby, Lolah got the keys to the suite that Sticks had booked online for her. Sticks had said that he would be there as soon as he could, but it would be at least two hours. She figured she might as well wait in style and comfort.

That bullshit with Carlos's wife popping up out of nowhere, accusing Lolah of fucking her man, had created major negative energy in her space. Lolah just wanted to decompress and regroup. She ordered a piece of chocolate cake and a bottle of wine from room service to smooth things out and take the edge off.

Half the bottle and several hours later, she heard a knock at the door. Just to be sure, Lolah asked, "Who's there?" She had had enough surprises for one night.

"Stop playing and let me in, baby girl." It was definitely Sticks to the rescue.

Once opening the door, she asked, "What took you so long?" It was after three in the morning.

"I told you that I was in the middle of something." He greeted her with a kiss on her cheek. "But I got here as soon as I could." Sticks's eyes scanned the suite, noting the half bottle of Chardonnay. "Nice room, and do you really need to be drinking?"

"Probably not, but after all the drama tonight and then having to wait hours for you, maybe I did."

He didn't play her game with her. Instead, he changed the subject. "Are you ready to bounce or do you want to chill for a while?"

Lolah took a seat on the bed wearing a pair of boy shorts and a T-shirt from the "you never know bag" that she always carried in her trunk for emergency purposes.

He took a seat beside her and asked, "So what happened?"

She put her hand up. "You are not going to believe this one," she said. "In fact, I'm going to insist that you let me pour you a drink for this one," she said as she got up to grab a glass.

His eyes followed her as she walked over to the glass. He took his shoes off while she was heading back over to him. "Damn, let me get comfortable."

She sat down beside him, put her legs on his and explained everything to him, a blow by blow of what happened with Carlos's wife. When she was done with talking about the whole scenario, she asked, "So what do you think?"

"I think that the next vehicle we get you is going to be an Escalade or a limo, with a hired driver. It hasn't even been six months yet and you have already gone through at least three vehicles. You've got to be more careful," he joked.

She stood up in front of him. "You a comedian now?" she asked, batting her eyelashes, with her hand on her hip, and her boy shorts were rocking a camel toe. "What you really thinking? Be real with me, tell me what is exactly on your mind, at this exact minute."

She could see how he was looking at her, "I don't know what I'm going to do with you?"

"Love me," she blurted out, letting the alcohol speak for her. "Why is that so hard."

"I do already," he said.

"I'm not talking about no sister love either."

He let out a slight chuckle. "I wish it was that simple." He went into deep thought.

"It is, and what? You mean you don't know what you gone do with me?" she asked more curious.

He was quiet for a second, wanting to make sure that he chose his words correctly. "I think that you are beautiful, and you are the type of chick I wish I could run across, and I like you . . . a lot. But I don't know how our Pops would feel about us being together like that."

"Honestly, it don't matter, we both grown," she said. "I know my Pops would only want happiness for me, and if you made me happy, then he would be happy. And you do." She kissed him on his cheek. But in the back of her mind she was thinking of Mickey's response to when she told him she had feelings for Sticks. Why had her news pissed him off?

"You know it's mad awkward for me 'cause I like you and every day that shit is growing."

"I like you too"—she looked into his eyes—"you don't feel the attraction here, because I do?"

"I do," he said with a slow nod. "I do."

She leaned in and kissed him and he kissed back and put his arm around her. She liked how warm his mouth felt as their tongues intertwined in each other's mouth. The long, intense kisses went on for over ten minutes and his manhood rose. He ran his hands up her legs and she was like a waterfall.

"You know we about to do something we can't take back," he whispered.

"I know," she said back, only wanting him inside of her.

"Everything changes from here," he reminded her.

"I know, I bet on us," Peaches said, "with no doubts and willing to risk it all."

Sticks nuzzled his chin against Peaches's lips. He knelt to the ground wrapping his arms around her waist, placing the perimeter of his face in her navel. His head went back and forth sideways. Sticks looked up at Peaches and said, "Let me take care of you, baby girl." He laid her on her back while his right hand massaged and caressed her nipples and lips to her inner region. Her body felt like it was suspended in air. Sticks's touch against her skin gave her shivers, and he was maneuvering around her body like he had an all-access pass to her desires. That's when he took her T-shirt and soaking wet boy shorts off and removed his own clothes, never taking his eyes off of her. As he stripped down, for a split second, she got a little intimidated, when saw that he was hung like a horse. His extremely large member rested in the middle of his thigh.

Damn, she thought to herself, then spoke out loud to him. "I don't know how I'm going to handle that," she admitted, not wanting to be a disappointment to him. She wanted more than anything to be able to please him.

"Don't worry," he said, "I will be easy with you." He positioned himself in between her legs, taking it slow, going in and out methodically to make his entry easy and pleasurable for her.

Once he was finally inside of her, his strokes were gentle and intense. She enjoyed every minute of their lovemaking. By the time she got used to his big Johnson being inside of her, and she started throwing it back at him, he reached his climax. He began shaking all over the place and announced, "I'm coming, baby."

"Come inside of me," she demanded, and he did.

18

Savoring the Moment

Sticks's strong arms were the only place Peaches wanted to be. Their night of lovemaking was absolutely unforgettable and had her emotions running wild. She was treasuring and savoring every moment.

However, it was after ten in the morning and her father had always stressed she be out of the bed by 9 a.m. He would say, "Only a broke person lies in the bed when the banks are opened. If you're out of the bed, your chances are better at putting some cash in or getting some out." She'd always taken this way of thinking seriously.

However, this day was different and that rule didn't apply. The truth of the matter was, neither Sticks nor her were broke and after the roller-coaster ride she had the day before, she deserved to enjoy the day off, doing nothing. She spent the next day in Sticks's arms, making love, talking, and watching On Demand movies. The feelings of mental and physical ecstasy that she had felt were unlike anything she had felt before. She had never really been in love before, and if this was love she was feeling, then at that very moment she understood the reason why such an emotion could make people do the crazy things they did. It was like a rush, a drug, a high.

The day had come and gone, and now it was nightfall again. Sticks set up a romantic midnight picnic on the beach. They made love under the stars, then decided to take the party back upstairs to their room. Once back upstairs, she had a sudden impulse, stepped outside of her and Sticks's magical world for a few minutes and grabbed her cell phone.

"Who you calling, baby?" Sticks asked when she grabbed her phone. He wanted to keep every second of her attention.

"Checking my messages," she said.

"I thought you weren't going to worry about anything until tomorrow morning," he reminded her.

"Just checking messages, babe. I won't return any calls until tomorrow, though. I promise."

"I don't really understand that, but okay, cool." With that being said, he grabbed his phone and checked his too.

Her voice mail was full. Damn near most were from Carlos apologizing for the ordeal with his wife, Millie. "I had no idea that she had followed me and had been watching us. And had followed you. My apologies, and I truly hope you don't let this affect our business."

As she listened, she spoke out loud. "I can't believe this, this is pure craziness."

"What?" Sticks asked. Then she put her phone on speakerphone so she could hear them. Then it got crazier as the next message came on.

"Bitch, I know you got some fucking nerve." She heard Lyle's voice. Her first thought was to not even listen to it, just delete it. But she decided to listen for shits and giggles. After all, what could Lyle say to really blow her high?

"You little hypocrite, the pot calling the kettle black," Lyle said in his highest pitched voice. "You had the gall to get furious with The Bombshell about my little ordeal and you wrapped all up in these love triangles and shit."

"What the fuck he talking about?" she asked, twisting her face up, not having the foggiest idea, but before she could get her thought out good enough, Lyle continued talking as to fill her in as if he wasn't talking to a machine and she was right there.

"Yes, Ms. Goody-Two-Shoes, I seen the billboards! That's right, and that picture of you, they could have took a better one."

Lolah's heart was in her undies.

Lyle continued, "I never took you as the type to mess with somebody's husband. But I should have known, it be bitches like you that do that kind of ratchet shit. But, honey, those billboards are lined up and down I-95 with your picture, name splattered all on it. Baby, you fucked the wrong woman's man, and let me be the first to tell you, it's just not a good look. Matter of fact, I'm going to send you a picture of it," he said before ending the message. "I gotta go have a drink for this tea honey I'm spilling. And after this mind-blowing gossip done came to light about you, Ms. Honey thing, you do owe me an apology and not on my voice mail either."

Lolah was undone and she was furious. If she was asleep,

it was time for somebody to wake her. She couldn't believe what was happening. She looked at her picture that Lyle had sent, and low and behold it was a picture of her with the words *home wrecker* written over it on a big-ass billboard.

"What in the fuck?" she said out loud. *"Is this really my life? I mean, really? How in the fuck could this really happen?"*

She sat dumbfounded for a second; then she called Carlos. But Sticks took the phone from her—"I will go deal with this"—and took her in her arms. "I promise it's going to be all right, baby. These billboards are going to be down in twenty-four hours. I promise you. This is some real bullshit." Sticks was angry but tried to keep calm because he knew that they both didn't need to be angry.

"How could this happen? How could she get this up so quick?" Peaches asked.

"But as quick as they got up, they will be taken down. I promise you," Sticks assured her.

Sticks taking charge calmed her down. She grabbed the remote. "You going to order another movie?" he asked.

"No, just find something to watch, see what's going on in this crazy city." She shook her head, trying to pull herself together.

"As late as it is, it's only infomercials," Sticks said as he listened to his messages.

Lolah took the remote control from him and kept channel surfing. "You are probably right."

When Sticks didn't respond, she focused her attention to him, but he had a solemn expression on his face. "What is it, babe?"

He didn't respond for a second; then she reminded him, "Remember, no secrets."

Now it was his turn to share his phone messages. He'd gotten one from Matteo. "Junior, I don't know what you two lovebirds are out there doing. Yeah, don't be surprised. I'm a long ways from stupid; I might be old, but I ain't blind. Even a blind man could see the feelings y'all two got, and it's so bittersweet. Anyways, I ain't call to lecture you on who to love. Shit done got complicated. Shit done hit the fan in so many different ways. This whole ordeal is turning into a freak show and on top of that Mickey is here with his shovel to dig up bones from the past. The son of a bitch drove here after he hung up from Lolah, and he's ready to lay all the cards on the table. Call me, son."

"What bones from the past, Sticks?" She wanted some answers. "What are the ties that bind? What happened? Tell me. Please tell me. Share with me," she practically begged.

"It's complicated," Sticks said. "I don't even know how to explain or where to begin." He shook his head, not knowing if they should wait for their fathers or if he should tell her his version of everything and how, exactly, their fathers are connected. He was quiet, mulling everything over.

"Sticks," she said, with a confused look on her face.

He took a deep breath, not knowing where to start to explain. So he started from the beginning. "When we were living back in Virginia, Mickey and Matteo were raised up in the same house like brothers. When they got older, they chose different paths of the game. Mickey was a junkie—"

"What are you talking about?" Peaches interrupted.

"Mickey wasn't ever no junkie. Your information must be wrong."

"This was a long time ago. But I'm telling the truth. He hustled for Matteo, and at that time Matteo was a big-time dealer who ran the city." Sticks took a deep breath, then continued. "You weren't even ten yet, so you wouldn't remember. I was fourteen, and I wanted a piece of the action. To prove myself to my father. But Matteo didn't want me in the game. Plus, I was too young. But I wouldn't listen.

"I dipped into some of my father's new shipment that he had just got in, and went to hit the block and started selling it. I had no idea that it was raw, uncut heroin when I sold it to Emma. . . ."

Peaches couldn't believe what she was hearing. Did he mean Emma, like her mother Emma, who died when Peaches was seven years old? Her mother and Mickey were junkies? And Matteo and Sticks were their suppliers? It was just too much to take. She could barely process the rest of what Sticks was saying.

"Emma shared it with two of her get-high buddies. They all died from an overdose. I was devastated and ashamed and swore I'd never try my hand at the drug business again. After Matteo saw what the life had done to us and how he had had such a negative influence in his community, he changed. He had always told himself that he was providing jobs for the felons and uneducated, but he never looked at it as the poison he was polluting his people's bodies and lives with. He had done collateral damage and hurt so many that he cared about, including Mickey, Emma, and especially me, his own son."

Peaches could see where this was going, so she filled in the rest of Sticks's story. "So Matteo wanted out, right? He took an early retirement, packed up, and made a home in Miami using his dope money to start up the new business. Since then neither of you have ever looked back. You put the past and everyone in Virginia behind you . . . until I showed up."

Sticks had girlfriends before, but none of them had an effect on him or his heart like Lolah did, and it was strange to him because it was such a short time. He asked himself, Was it lust? Then answered, No, couldn't be. Was it infatuation? No, he knew the difference. It was definitely love.

Sticks had no idea if she would ever forgive him, but he knew getting the past off his chest was the only way to move forward. He closed his eyes, afraid to look in Peaches's eyes and see her feelings for him turn to hate.

"Sticks," Peaches called out, trying to convince him to allow her to enter into his deep thoughts with him.

Sticks sat quiet. This was the first time in his adult life that he was faced with a situation that he didn't know how to handle. "Give me a second, baby," he said to try to sort things out in his head.

And that's when Lolah caught a glimpse of the television. "Oh my goodness," she said out loud, breaking his thoughts and forcing him to focus on her as she raised up out of the bed to her feet and was glued to the television.

There she was, Peaches Brown, that same picture that they had taken off of Malika's Instagram page. She couldn't believe that she was on *America's Most Wanted*. Maybe they had shown it earlier in the day, and this was a replay. She didn't know, but all she knew was she couldn't breathe, and she felt like she was back in Virginia in Tony's back room on the poker table with his hands reaching for her belt trying to take off her pants. She wanted to maintain a poker face, but she couldn't breathe. She felt like the walls were closing in on her.

Sticks came to her side, trying to comfort her.

She could not believe she had been hit with the triple whammy, first the billboards, then Sticks's part in her mother's death, and now this. The necklace that Carlos had given her, maybe it wasn't blessed, maybe it was cursed.

She didn't look anything like that picture anymore, but she was now afraid that it wouldn't take long before someone would put two and two together.

"They are closing in on me," she said to Sticks. As she looked into his eyes, she put the past in the past. He wasn't the kid who'd made a terrible mistake that killed her mother; he was now a man she could trust with her life.

"No, they are not," he said. "Real talk, no one would even notice you."

Tears came to her eyes. For the first time in a very long time, she cried as Sticks took her in his arms. She didn't utter a word but knew that her Miami gig was up.

Just when she thought that Miami was home and her life was coming together, all hell breaks loose. She was back at square one.

Leaving her father, friends, business, and mother's resting place was the hardest thing she ever had to do. And now she had to do the same thing all over again. Naturally, she thought that if she had to ever leave, it would be easier each time, but the game had definitely changed. There were emotional ties and leaving Sticks and Matteo and Miami strangely was still going to be just as hard.

But she couldn't think about the good-byes right now. She needed a new plan. She looked up at Sticks and remembered their conversation back on Ocean Drive, about using her skills to create a new persona. She didn't know if her new life would include Sticks, but she had an idea that would free her from the most wanted list for good—a disguise so fabulous there was only one place she'd fit in—the city of sin!

Available now wherever books are sold!

Dirty Rotten Liar: The Misadventures of Mink LaRue
by Noire
What can go wrong when con-mami Mink LaRue joins forces with her slick-tongued look-alike Dy-Nasty Jenkins to run a hustle on the super-rich Dominion oil family?

Playing Dirty
by Kiki Swinson
By bribing cops and officials, sleeping with her boss, and convincing her friend in the DEA to make evidence disappear, Yoshi Lomax has become a top criminal defense attorney. But when she takes the case of a badass Haitian mob boss, an unknown enemy begins sabotaging her every move. . . .

One Night Stand
by Kendall Banks
Single and sexy, Zaria Hopkins always gets what she wants. And what she wants is Gerald Hardy. But for this cheating husband and father, the hookup with Zaria was just a one-night thing. Now Zaria's betrayed heart seeks revenge, and she'll do whatever it takes to get it. . . .

In De'nesha Diamond's explosive series, the fiercest ride-or-die chicks in Memphis are battling alongside—and against—their ruthless men to be the last diva standing.

GANGSTA DIVAS
On sale now

1

Lucifer

"NOOOOOOOOOOOOOOOOOOO!"
The light. Where is the light in Mason's eyes? The world tilts off its axis as my brain forces my heart to accept the unbelievable. *He's dead.* The leader of the Memphis Vice Lords . . . my lover, my best friend . . . my life—dead. Flipped upside down in a black Escalade on the side of the highway, I'm twisted in an awkward position. It feels like every damn bone in my body is broken. Still I scream until my voice fails and my lungs beg for oxygen.

My world.

My rock.

Since we were kids, I've been Mason's ride-or-die chick—not because of the shared allegiance with the Vice Lord family, but because I loved the air he breathed and the ground he walked on.

Until recently, he didn't know about the torch I carried for him. To him, I was his right-hand bitch, blasting and carving niggas up who dared to cross the Vice Lord family. I never realized that my brother Bishop had cock-blocked my ass and made it clear with his best friend that I was off-limits. All that shit changed when that crooked-ass cop Melanie Johnson got murked and all her secrets fell out of the closet. The bitch had some kind of hold on him—and apparently Mason's life-long sworn enemy, Python, too. She had even convinced Mason that she was carrying his child.

I knew the bitch was no good and was more than thrilled when Mason realized where his heart truly belonged—with me.

His world.

His rock.

A couple of hours ago we made love for the first time. Hell, there's still a sweet soreness throbbing between my legs that if I close my eyes I can still feel him.

Rare tears fuck up my vision and splash over my lashes as I try to accept the unacceptable.

He's gone.

This shit wasn't supposed to go down like this. We had planned everything. Everything.

Hit the Pink Monkey, blow that shit up.

Hit Goodson Construction, mow down every Gangster Disciple in sight.

The hitch: Python's ass was nowhere to be found.

Bishop fucked up. He was the one who'd been in charge

of tagging that nigga. Instead of hitting the chief, we got his second-in-command, McGriff. Turned out his ass was cutting his own deal with their supplier behind Python's back, tryna come up. We did that muthafucka a favor takin' them out.

That shit didn't sit well with Mason.

Hyped on a murderous high, we made up a new plan on the fly and drove our murder train toward the heart of the Gangster Disciples: Shotgun Row.

The shit was bold. Any other time, we would've known it was a suicide mission. We were picked off a few miles out. Bullets flew like we were in the Middle East. By chance we spotted Python. We chased that ass going the wrong way on the highway. We were gaining ground until a near head-on collision with an eighteen-wheeler spun and then flipped us off the road.

"Muthafucka, answer me! What the fuck is your real name?" Python, the chief nigga of the Gangster Disciples, roars at Mason. They are inches outside the flipped vehicle where the nigga was just wailing his meaty fist against Mason's jaw. Both gangsta chiefs are physically intimidating men. Their major differences are that Python is covered in tats and has a surgically altered tongue so that it resembled one of a snake. Mason, a little bulkier, a little darker, shiny on top with a goatee and one fucked up eye that he lost in a gun battle years ago. Despite these differences, I'm suddenly hit with the realization that at this angle these two look eerily similar.

"ANSWER ME," Python roars.

"G-get away from him," I spit, ignoring the taste of my

own blood. However, the pain ricocheting throughout my body intensifies to the point that I know I'm on the verge of blacking out. I don't care. I need to protect my man at all cost.

Then this nigga does something that surprises the shit out of me. The muthafucka starts crying. I ain't talking about a few bullshit sniffles either. It's a gut-wrenching roar of a wounded lion.

BOOM! BOOM!

The heavens crack with thunder and lightning flashes across the sky. A second later, rain falls in torrential sheets as Python tucks his head into the crook of Mason's neck and weeps.

"I didn't know," he croaks. "I didn't know."

I'm numb all over except where my heart feels like it's being chiseled out of my chest. I don't understand what the fuck I'm looking at and I ain't too sure that I'm not imagining this shit. Tears? From this big, overgrown nigga who thinks his ass is a snake?

Nobody is going to believe this shit, especially since the war between the Vice Lords and the Gangster Disciples has been raging decades before any of us burst onto the scene. But no two gang leaders have ever beefed harder than Mason and Python. It's like the world demands that there can only be one.

"Forgive me," Python sobs. "Please forgive me."

BOOM! BOOM!

This nigga has lost it. I redouble my efforts and after a hell of a lot of huffing and puffing, I'm able to move my arm about an inch. It's not much, but my fingertips brush the barrel of Mason's TEC-9. *I can do it. I can do it.*

I don't know why this muthafucka is crying and I really don't give a shit. I'm more interested in street justice. An eye for an eye. A life for a life.

I take pride in being the baddest bitch breathing so it's killing me that the pain seizing me right now is getting the best of me. Darkness encroaches my peripheral and a new desperation takes hold of me. *I can't black out now. I can't.* I know at my core that I'll never be able to forgive myself if I don't take this human reptile out.

BOOM! BOOM!

Chugging in a deep breath, my nose burns from the stench of gasoline. *Is this muthafucka about to blow up?* It takes everything I have to twist my head around, but everywhere I turn, the smell grows stronger until it feels like my nose hairs are on fire.

Fuck it. If it blows, it blows. The three of us can blaze up and that shit is just fine with me. In fact, I prefer it. I won't have to return to Ruby Cove with my tail tucked between my legs and buzzing whispers about how my gangsta wasn't tight enough to protect our leader. Niggas will look for any excuse to try to knock a bitch off her throne. But if we all go out together, we'll become legends in the streets. I close my eyes and allow death to seduce me.

A sob lodges in my throat, forcing me to choke on the son of a bitch. Hell, I can't tell what hurts more, my broken body or my broken heart.

Regardless, if death is coming, the bitch is slow.

BOOM! BOOM!

A spark. My eyes fly open. I need a spark to set this shit off. My gaze darts around again for something—*anything* that can make a spark.

"I didn't know. I didn't know," Python sobs again, clinging tighter to Mason.

What the fuck did this nigga not know? My gaze returns to the two gangstas, but what I see does nothing to clear up my confusion. Either I banged my head too hard or I'm seeing that this nigga really is broken up about taking his longtime enemy out. Soaked to the bone, Python has wrapped Mason in his arms and is rocking back and forth—much like I would do, if I could get my ass to move.

BOOM! BOOM!

My brain flies back to the TEC-9. If I can get one shot off, I can end all this bullshit. I draw in another deep breath to build up my resolve, but the strong scent of gasoline now has waves of bile crashing around in my gut and burning up my esophagus. Choking on my own vomit is not the way I'd pictured exiting the game.

At the last second, I'm able to roll onto my side and hurl. But even that shit feels like I'm hawking up gobs of broken glass. Before long, I'm swimming in acidic bile.

"I'm taking you home," I catch Python saying through the booming thunder and hammering rain. Next, he awkwardly struggles to pick Mason up.

"Wait. No!" I choke on more bile. "What are you doing?"

He ignores me as he struggles to stand on the wet earth. After splashing around, he hooks his arms underneath Mason's and then locks his fingers across his chest so that he can drag him away from the vehicle. If he succeeds it will fuck up my plan.

BOOM! BOOM!

Clenching my jaw tight and holding my breath, I force myself to calm down. For my troubles, my stomach revolts and cramps up.

Move your ass! Move your ass! I thrust my hand up again to reach that damn semiautomatic. Again, my fingertips brush the barrel.

"C'mon, Willow. C'mon." I twist and squirm while Python succeeds in dragging Mason from view. "NOOOOOOO!" Fat tears roll over my lashes at a clip that blinds my ass. I redouble my efforts, but I . . . just . . . can't reach this muthafucka.

BOOM! BOOM!

I can't block out the horrific images of what the Gangster Disciples will do to Mason's body once Python gets it back to his home turf. Everything from chopping him up, pissing and shitting on him and even sexually molesting him, crosses my mind. I know how the GDs get down and that's not the way Mason deserves to be taken out.

"Oh God, baby. I'm so sorry." Something snaps within me and tears that I've been holding back for decades pour out of me. I'm not a crier. I never cry. But this shit has broken me. I can't imagine a world without my nigga. I never thought I had to.

BOOM! BOOM!

I close my eyes and hear the opening and closing of a car door. Less than ten seconds later, an engine roars to life and tires squeal in a growing pool of wet earth. My sobs grow more pathetic and no mental military barking can get my ass to stop.

I fucked up.

I fucked up.

I fucked up.

That shit repeats in my head for I don't know how long before I hear another vehicle pull off to the side of the road. Even then I don't know or even give a shit who the hell it is. I want to be left alone in my own private hell until I die from my car injuries or from my shattered heart.

"WILLOW," Bishop yells, cutting through the bullshit cluttering my head. "Willow, are you fucking in there?"

BOOM! BOOM!

I battle myself on whether to answer. To try and save myself after this colossal fuck-up seems too much like a bitch move.

"WILLOW!"

I squeeze my eyes tight and will my brother to go away.

"WILLOW!"

The desperation in his voice tears at me. The sibling beefs we've had in our lives are so fucking small in the grand scheme of things. If a gun was pressed to my head to name someone who has loved me unconditionally my entire life, the name I'd spit would be: Bishop. I followed him and Mason into this game like an irritating pest and I forged my moniker in the street with the big dawgs—not the Flowers. I didn't want to just lock down a big lieutenant and play wifey. I wanted to be the big lieutenant and tell the world to suck my balls.

I succeeded. My people love me but more importantly

they respect my ass. There's never a question of whether I can hold shit down. But after tonight, will that change?

BOOM! BOOM!

"Death, where are you?" I beg softly. "Take me out of this place."

"Here she is," Bishop shouts.

My eyes spring back open and I see Bishop's scared face through the shattered glass of the front window. The second our eyes connect, I see hope ripple across his chiseled face.

"Don't worry, Willow. We're going to get you out of there."

That's what the fuck I'm afraid of.

"Hold on." Bishop hops back onto his feet and calls out to the other members of our fam. "Y'all niggas, c'mon over here and help me get her out of here!"

"No." Weakly, I shake my head. It's all I can do since I lack the strength to beg him to let me die.

BOOM! BOOM!

As the storm rages on, I pick up the faint sound of wailing police sirens.

"C'mon, nigga. We need to hurry this shit up," Bishop barks.

"Grab her feet and pull her out this way," Novell, I think, shouts.

When he grabs the bottom of my foot, I roar, "AAAAARRRRRGGGH," and nearly burst my own damn eardrums.

"NIGGA, STOP!" Bishop snatches Novell back. "What the fuck is wrong with you?"

"What?"

"Are you blind or some shit? Look at her fuckin' leg.

Can't you see that we can't pull her out that way? Look at her leg."

BOOM! BOOM!

What the hell is wrong with my leg? I try to peek, but I can't even swivel my head around. I need to rest. *I'm tired— so fuckin' tired.* My eyes lower and though I can still hear the shit that's going on around me, I can't say that I give a fuck about any of it.

Sirens grow louder while the booming thunder shakes everything around me.

BOOM! BOOM!

"Kick out the front window and grab her that way," Bishop yells. A second later, I hear their Timberlands attack the glass. Next, several hands grab my arms and drag me out of my gasoline-drenched coffin and into the freezing downpour where my tears blend in with the rain.